"I want you to tell me the truth, Maggie,"

Colin said grimly.

Madaline's breath locked in her lungs. "Go away."

He stood rigid. "Maybe I should leave. I'll find my answers some other way."

A fresh rush of panic swept through her. "No!"

"I will find out what's going on," he assured her, then added, "I promise you that whatever you tell me will be held in strictest confidence." He scowled at her obvious indecision. "I would never do anything to bring harm to you," he said gruffly. "But I want to know what's going on and I *will* find out."

She saw the determined line of his jaw. "If you don't want to cause me any grief, then you will forget this matter and not mention it to anyone."

He took a step toward her. Cupping her face in his hands, he forced her to look up at him. "You are still a virgin, aren't you?"

Dear Reader,

It's that time of year again—pink hearts, red roses and sweet dreams abound as we celebrate that most amorous of holidays—St. Valentine's Day!

Silhouette Romance captures the sentimental mood of the month with six new tales of lovers who are meant for each other—and even if *they* don't realize it from the start, *you* will!

Last month, we launched our new FABULOUS FATHERS series with the first heartwarming tale of fatherhood. Now, we bring you the second title in the series, *Uncle Daddy.* Popular author Kasey Michaels has packed this story with humor and emotion as hero Gabe Logan learns to be a father—and a husband.

Also in February, Elizabeth August's *The Virgin Wife* whisks you away to Smytheshire, a fictional town where something dark and secret is going on. Once you've been there, you'll want to visit this wonderful, intriguing place again—and you can! Be sure to look for other Smytheshire books coming in the near future from Elizabeth August and Silhouette Romance.

To complete this month's offerings, we have book one of Laurie Paige's new ALL-AMERICAN SWEETHEARTS series, *Cara's Beloved,* as well as *To the Rescue* by Kristina Logan, *Headed for Trouble* by Joan Smith and Marie Ferrarella's *Babies on His Mind.*

In months to come, we'll be bringing you books by all your favorite authors—Diana Palmer, Annette Broadrick, Suzanne Carey and more! In the meantime, we at Silhouette Romance wish you a Happy Valentine's Day spent with someone special!

Anne Canadeo
Senior Editor

THE VIRGIN WIFE

Elizabeth August

Published by Silhouette Books New York
America's Publisher of Contemporary Romance

To Susie, Lee, Lillie, Sondra, Myra, Debbie, Terry and Linda for planning wonderful family picnics.

SILHOUETTE BOOKS
300 E. 42nd St., New York, N.Y. 10017

THE VIRGIN WIFE

ISBN: 0-373-08921-X

First Silhouette Books printing February 1993

Printed in the U.S.A.

Books by Elizabeth August

Silhouette Romance

Author's Choice #554
Truck Driving Woman #590
Wild Horse Canyon #626
Something So Right #668
The Nesting Instinct #719
Joey's Father #749
Ready-Made Family #771
The Man from Natchez #790
A Small Favor #809
The Cowboy and the Chauffeur #833
Like Father, Like Son #857
The Wife He Wanted #881
**The Virgin Wife* #921

*Smytheshire, Mass.

A Note From The Author:

I've lived in both large cities and small towns. I confess, I loved the towns best. Every community, large or small, has its eccentrics and its secrets. But I've always felt that in a town these elements become more focused. They add a touch of spice or, in some cases, discord, that seems to permeate the air and give the town a personality uniquely its own. When the thought occurred to me of creating an outwardly normal, conservative, rural community founded on a secret known to only a few but affecting the majority—a secret that in itself could be the basis for eccentricities—I found this too interesting a concept to resist. Thus, Smytheshire and its residents began to take form in my mind.

I have to admit, I've been shocked by how alive the people of Smytheshire have become to me. I've had a lot of fun creating these books. I hope you will enjoy reading them as much as I've enjoyed writing them.

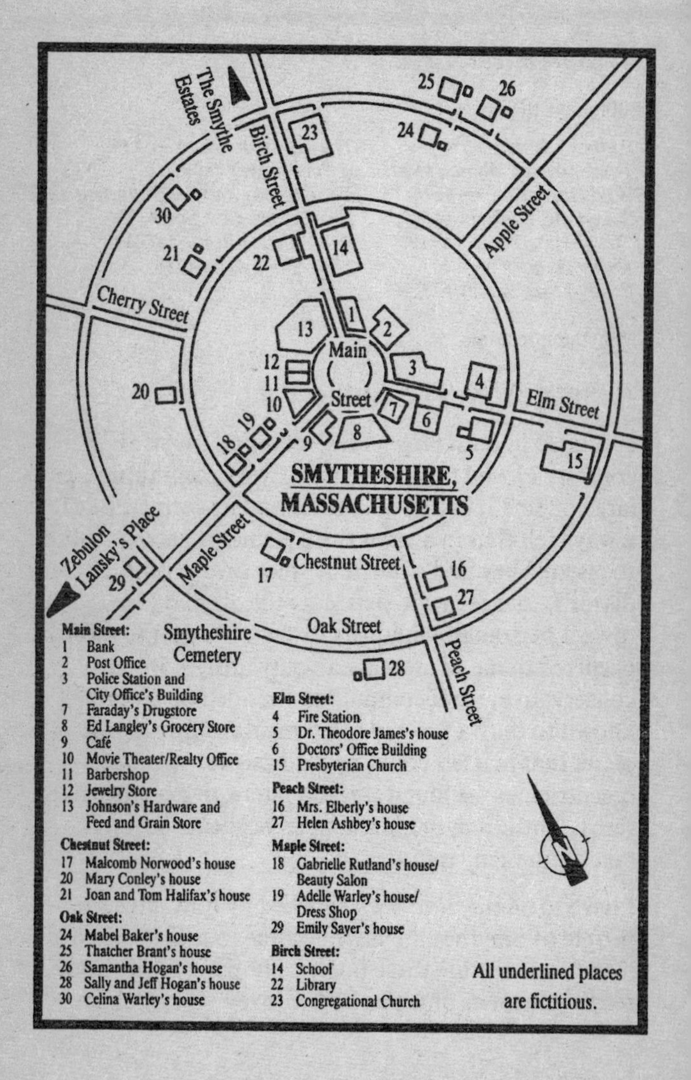
The Smythe Estates
Birch Street
Apple Street
Cherry Street
Main Street
Elm Street
SMYTHESHIRE, MASSACHUSETTS
Zebulon Lansky's Place
Maple Street
Chestnut Street
Oak Street
Peach Street
Smytheshire Cemetery
Main Street:
1 Bank
2 Post Office
3 Police Station and City Office's Building
7 Faraday's Drugstore
8 Ed Langley's Grocery Store
9 Café
10 Movie Theater/Realty Office
11 Barbershop
12 Jewelry Store
13 Johnson's Hardware and Feed and Grain Store
Chestnut Street:
17 Malcomb Norwood's house
20 Mary Conley's house
21 Joan and Tom Halifax's house
Oak Street:
24 Mabel Baker's house
25 Thatcher Brant's house
26 Samantha Hogan's house
28 Sally and Jeff Hogan's house
30 Celina Warley's house
Elm Street:
4 Fire Station
5 Dr. Theodore James's house
6 Doctors' Office Building
15 Presbyterian Church
Peach Street:
16 Mrs. Elberly's house
27 Helen Ashbey's house
Maple Street:
18 Gabrielle Rutland's house/ Beauty Salon
19 Adelle Warley's house/ Dress Shop
29 Emily Sayer's house
Birch Street:
14 School
22 Library
23 Congregational Church
N
All underlined places are fictitious.

Chapter One

"Virginity can be hazardous to your health," a gruff whispery voice intoned into Madaline MacGreggor-Smythe's ear.

Stunned, she stood momentarily frozen, her knuckles whitening as she gripped the telephone receiver. Then the line went dead. As if the instrument were burning her, she dropped the receiver into its cradle.

The morning sun coming through the window glinted off her wedding band. How could anyone know her marriage had never been consummated? she wondered in a rush of panic. *They couldn't,* came the answer. "Don't overreact," she cautioned herself.

Normally she maintained a calm control over herself. But lately life had been a strain. Outsiders, those from busy metropolises, would probably wonder what could possibly have a resident of the sleepy little town of Smytheshire on edge. This rural community, situated in the mountainous region of northwestern Massachusetts, with a population of just over fifteen hundred, was the image of a peaceful American town. "Well, we have our secrets just like everyone else," Madaline muttered. "And I didn't need a call like that to start my day."

A shiver of apprehension shook her as her gaze focused on her diamond engagement ring. It was too large, she thought for the zillionth time. Her attention shifted to the gold band beside it. No one could possibly know the truth, she assured herself again.

The call was most likely a practical joke and her number had been dialed at random, she reasoned, noting that the caller had not addressed her by name. This conviction grew stronger as she remembered the rash of threatening phone calls a few years back that had followed the opening of a horror movie. The plot of the film had involved a practical joke that had backfired on the participants. The morning after the first showing of the movie, half the townsfolk had gotten phone calls from a person who said, "I know what you did and I'm going to tell." Several people had been very shaken. Joe Barley had actually confessed his infidelity to his wife, which had led to two divorces; he'd cheated on her with a married woman whose husband was not happy to learn of his wife's unfaithfulness.

Madaline hadn't been amused then, and she wasn't now.

Scowling, she crossed to the front door. The phone had been ringing when she'd entered, and in the rush to reach it, she'd left her keys in the lock. As she removed them and closed the door, another wave of apprehension swept over her. She shrugged as if that could shake off the feeling of uneasiness. Normally she felt totally comfortable and at ease within these walls. This two-story, white frame house belonged to her. It had been the home she'd grown up in. After her mother's death, she'd inherited it. Now she used it as her place of business. Madaline MacGreggor, Architect, the sign out front read.

"It's this latest project I've been working on—it's destroyed the tranquillity of my life," she admitted grimly. That she had been talking aloud to herself for the past few minutes was testament to the frayed state of her nerves.

As she started toward her office, she paused in front of the large mirror that hung across from her receptionist-secretary's desk in the wide entrance foyer. Madaline rarely thought about her sex appeal, but she suddenly found herself making a critical assessment. She had a nicely featured face. Not gorgeous, but certainly passable. Her thick long burgundy hair was held back by a pale green scarf tied like a ribbon. The style gave her a casual, carefree air. For one brief moment she wished she *felt* that carefree. It suddenly seemed like a long time since she'd laughed.

Frowning at this thought, she returned to her examination. The pale green scarf matched the linen suit she was wearing—both enhanced the green of her eyes. The suit was tailored for a woman's figure and it fitted her well. The straight skirt modestly gave evidence of femininely rounded hips. The jacket nipped in snugly at her small waist, a style that emphasized her full bustline. Her gaze shifted to her lips. She licked them nervously, as she recalled being drawn into the warm depths of a pair of mahogany brown eyes, while a husky male voice told her he'd never seen a pair of lips that looked more sensual or inviting. Her body trembled, and she shoved the memory back into the dark recesses where it belonged. "Your mind really is going far afield these days," she grumbled at the image in the mirror.

Jerking her gaze away, she strode into the living room that now served as her office. She'd meant to go to her desk and check her messages. Instead she continued to her drawing table, where she stood looking down at the blueprints of a house. There was no doubt in her mind that it was *this* house that had her nerves on edge, had her overreacting to what was obviously a childish practical joke and had her thinking about her sex appeal. Madaline's fingers traced the white lines on the dark blue paper. They were the designs for a comfortable two-story, three-bedroom home—a home very like one she'd talked about designing four years earlier.

She'd been twenty-one at the time and still had one year of college to complete. Again the brown-eyed man's image filled her mind. He'd been twenty-five and strongly built from a life of hard physical labor. His father had run a small construction company that specialized in roofing, additions and general home repairs. From the time the man whose image still haunted her had been old enough to lift a hammer, he'd worked beside his father. He wasn't classically handsome. But he had eyes that seemed to see into her soul, and his lips had looked as sensual to her as hers had to him. His nose was slightly crooked from having been broken. Hot tears suddenly burned behind Madaline's eyes. The fracture had occurred when he'd been defending her, making that particular feature very dear to her. But that was in the past. That was when she'd thought she could trust him. Angrily she shoved his image out of her mind. That it had remained so vivid after all this time astonished her. He'd left town more than three years ago and she hadn't seen him since.

"And if I never see him again, I'll die happy. There are some things it would be best to forget," she said, her tone carrying an order that she should heed these words.

"Talking to yourself already?" a female voice asked from the doorway.

Glancing over her shoulder, Madaline saw her secretary, Samantha Hogan, entering. Samantha was in her late twenties and single. Being single, Madaline knew, was Samantha's choice. She'd had suitors, but none had captured her heart. Thick black hair framed her face. It was not a face that anyone would classify as beautiful, but it had a quality that garnered second looks from several of the available men in town. Most important to Madaline, Samantha had a cheerful disposition along with being efficient, reliable and highly organized. "It's been an unusual morning," Madaline hedged, wondering how much Samantha had heard and making a mental note to start closing her office door before she conducted any more private conversations with herself.

"What did you forget?" her secretary asked. "Is it something I can go get for you?" She laughed lightly. "There are mornings when I'd forget my head if it wasn't attached."

"It's nothing important," Madaline replied, relieved Samantha had only caught the very end of her self-scolding and had no real idea what it was about.

For a moment a look of indecisiveness came over Samantha's face, then she said hesitantly, "I had a sort of curious experience this morning."

Madaline began to pat herself on the back. No doubt Samantha had received one of the ridiculous phone calls, too.

"For some reason my grandmother's Ouija board caught my attention. I guess I was missing her. Anyway, I found myself playing with it," Samantha continued.

Madaline experienced a rush of disappointment. She also felt a twinge of sympathy for her secretary. For Samantha's sake, Madaline had hoped old Ada Hogan's interest in the Ouija board had not rubbed off on her granddaughter. The kinder townsfolk had considered the elderly woman eccentric. The rest had simply thought she was crazy. Most had considered it prudent to avoid her whenever possible.

Samantha flushed as if she could read Madaline's mind. "I know you don't believe in that kind of stuff, and I know nearly everyone thought my grandmother was a bit peculiar because she was so involved in it." Samantha's flush deepened. "I have to admit there were times when I wondered about her myself. But every once in a while the messages she received were surprisingly accurate." As if afraid she might lose her courage, she hurried on, "Anyway, I had an urge to play with her board this morning. It spelled out your name and then advised you to practice caution."

Mentally Madaline groaned. She'd hoped to gain proof that the call was a hoax, thus putting her mind at ease. Instead, she was receiving a warning from an amateur fortune-teller. "I'll remember not to walk under any ladders," she replied, wishing she'd pulled the covers up over her head and stayed in bed.

Samantha shifted uncomfortably. "I just thought I should mention it."

Madaline did not usually preach, but she liked her secretary and didn't want to see Samantha develop the same sort of reputation Ada had garnered. "If I remember correctly, shortly after your grandmother died and you inherited her Ouija board, you warned your sister, Joan, not to go on any trips for a month or so. On that advice, she canceled a trip to visit Tom's parents. They were upset because they'd been looking forward to seeing Tom and the kids. Tom and the kids were upset because they were looking forward to going fishing with his dad. In fact, everyone got angry at Joan for listening to you. Then a couple of weeks later, you were forced to admit you'd made a mistake and it would have been perfectly all right for her to travel."

Samantha's face reddened with acute embarrassment. "That was a disaster," she conceded, adding defensively, "I've never been very successful at using the board, and I would never have even tried except that Joan asked me to. And after that fiasco, I did swear I would never use the board again.'' Her gray eyes suddenly darkened like the sky before a storm. ''But that mistake wasn't entirely my fault. I'd had a run-in with our local chief of police, Thatcher Brant. That man can be the most irritating person.'' She shrugged exaggeratedly, as if just the thought of him caused her extreme discomfort.

Madaline regarded her secretary dryly. Thatcher was also a native-born resident of their town. He was about three years older than Samantha, and the two of them had been feuding since childhood. ''I thought you usually crossed the street when you saw the chief coming.''

''I usually do,'' Samantha replied. ''Anyway, I was still unnerved by the argument I'd had with him when I used the board. My grandmother used to caution me that, for the board to be truly accurate, the user should be calm and in a relaxed state.'' Apology returned to her face. ''You're right. I should stay away from it.''

''I think that would be for the best,'' Madaline concurred.

''Definitely for the best.'' Samantha looked thoroughly chastened. ''I'll just leave you to your work,'' she added, backing out of Madaline's office and pulling the door closed.

Alone once more, Madaline returned her gaze to the blueprints spread out on her drawing board. Her finger was resting on the mudroom just off the kitchen. This room was to have stone flooring so that on rainy days the children who lived in the house could enter there. A hard knot of regret formed in her stomach. Sharply turning her attention away from the plans, she paced across the room and stood staring out a back window at the small private garden beyond. It was silly to be behaving this way toward a drawing, she admonished herself.

But it wasn't just the plans for the house. It was the location, as well. Her client had talked old Zebulon Lanksy into selling the forty-eight acres that included Sanctuary Ridge. Madaline frowned. Only she and one other person had ever known the rock outcropping by that name. The image of the brown-eyed man again filled her mind.

"It's being up on that ridge again that's caused these memories to be so persistent," she grumbled, furious that she couldn't vanquish these particular thoughts of the past. There had been a time when she and the man had planned to build a home on the exact spot this house she was designing was to be constructed. When she'd discovered that was to be her client's location, she'd considered refusing the commission. But, she'd told herself, that would be cowardly. "However, a little cowardliness might have been good in this instance," she admitted with a wistful sigh, then frowned at herself again for this weakness.

The buzzer on her intercom caused her to jump slightly. Relieved to have something other than her memories to occupy her mind, she answered it.

"Mr. Phillips is here to see you," Samantha announced.

Madaline thought she heard an unusual note in her secretary's voice. *It's probably just my imagination,* she decided. This had been a very unsettling morning. "Send him in," she instructed. Richard Phillips was the client for whom she had designed the house. And the sooner she was finished with this project, the better, she affirmed mentally.

"Good morning, Madaline," Richard said with a smile as he entered her office and closed the door behind him.

He was a prominent Boston lawyer in his midfifties. His tall lean form was clothed in a navy blue, three-piece, pinstriped suit—a gold watch chain strung across the front of his vest. With his dark hair graying at the temples, he looked every inch the distinguished big-city lawyer, Madaline thought.

"Good morning." She returned his smile. "I've prepared the final plans. Once they have your okay, we can begin breaking ground."

A sheepishness came over his features. "I've a confession to make."

Maybe he's changed his mind, Madaline hoped. After all, Boston was a long drive from Smytheshire. And there was nothing exciting about this little town. Even as a weekend retreat, Richard Phillips would probably find Smytheshire too boring for his taste.

"The truth is, this house isn't for me. I've been acting for a client."

A surge of renewed apprehension shook Madaline. "A client?"

"I figured you might turn down the job if you knew it was for me," a male voice said from the doorway.

Madaline stared at the man who had just entered her office. She wanted to speak, but her vocal chords refused to work. He'd changed since he'd left town nearly four years ago. He looked older, more mature, the lines in his face harsher. And his dark brown eyes were guarded and cold.

"It's been a long time, Maggie," he said, his gaze not leaving her as he closed the door behind him. His jaw tensed, giving it a decidedly angular line. She remembered how he used to do that when something irritated him. "Mrs. Smythe," he corrected.

It was almost imperceivable. Someone who did not know him well would have missed it entirely. But she caught the veiled accusation in his voice. Her back stiffened. He had no right to condemn her!

"Madaline, this is my client, Colin Darnell," Richard said, watching the two of them dubiously.

"Mr. Darnell." Madaline congratulated herself. Her acknowledgment of the introduction had come out crisp and businesslike. There was no evidence in her voice of the shakiness she was feeling inside. She did not, however, extend her hand to him in greeting as she normally would have with any other client. She called herself a coward, but she was not ready for physical contact. She noticed he didn't seem interested in shaking her hand, either. He was wearing slacks with a turtleneck cotton shirt and a sports jacket. The shirt fit snugly and she could see that his physique had remained muscular. His hands were slid halfway into the pockets of his slacks, giving his posture a casual look. But there was nothing casual or even friendly about the cold inspection he was giving her.

She's changed, Colin thought. There was no laughter in those green eyes of hers. Of course seeing him again could account for that. He hadn't expected her to be pleased when he reappeared in her life. But it was more than just the eyes. Her bearing had none of that slightly uncertain self-conscious girlishness left in it. Instead, she looked like a mature woman who had decided what she wanted out of life and gone for it. *Which is precisely what she did,* he reminded himself. For the umpteenth time, he found himself cynically wondering if her high social position and all of her husband's wealth had brought her happiness. Again his jaw tensed. *She has a right to make her own choices,* he told himself. "Have you added the final changes I requested?" he asked brusquely, diverting his attention to the blueprints on her drawing board.

"Why me?" Madaline clamped her mouth shut on the last syllable. She'd meant to respond with a level businesslike "yes." She couldn't believe she'd blurted out that question. Granted, it was uppermost in her mind, but she'd never meant to let him guess the unnerving effect his unexpected appearance was having on her.

Colin experienced a small twinge of pleasure that he'd managed to rattle her. Then he scowled at himself. He'd come here to exorcise old memories, not to seek reprisal. "Because I knew you'd design the house I wanted," he responded with the pat answer he'd practiced. "Also, I need someone here in Smytheshire to keep an eye on the construction and see that it's done properly. And, since I've lost touch with most of the people here, I figured you'd know which locals would do a first-rate job." His gaze narrowed on her. "You were never one to settle for second-best."

Again she caught the hint of accusation in his voice. Rebellion filled her, but she refused to allow her control to slip again. She met his gaze with cool dignity. "I believe in quality."

He wanted to ask her if her husband met all of her expectations of "quality," but held back. Her answer, he was certain, would be a resounding yes. An image of Madaline's husband filled Colin's mind. Devin Smythe was Colin's age. As boys they'd never been friends. Devin's wealth had set him apart from most of the population of Smytheshire, and he had seemed to prefer to keep that distance. But, Colin had to admit, Devin had never flaunted his affluence. He had been, as a general rule, mild-mannered and polite in all of his dealings with others.

Of course there had been the incident with the puppy. It had occurred during the summer Colin and Devin were ten. Joe Henly's purebred collie had had a litter. He usually sold the pups for a healthy price, but because Colin had helped him build a new pen and been there to assist during the delivery, Joe was going to give him one of the offspring as payment. The day the puppies were weaned and ready to leave their mother, Colin had gone over to

Joe's house. Devin was there to purchase one of the pups for his father as a birthday gift.

Joe had been on the phone when they'd arrived and had sent Devin and Colin down to the pen to take a look at the dogs. The runt of the litter seemed to take an instant dislike to Devin. As the two boys entered the pen, the puppy started yapping at Devin, then ran up and nipped him on the ankle. A look of fury flashed across Devin's features and he kicked the small furry bundle across the pen. Colin watched in shock. He never would have believed Devin could act so callously.

As the puppy shakily rose to its feet, Devin moved toward it. But instead of remorse, Colin saw malice in Devin's eyes. Fear for the little dog swept through him. Moving swiftly, he blocked Devin's path. "Don't touch that puppy," he warned threateningly.

Fury that Colin had the nerve to interfere showed on Devin's face. Then in the blink of an eye, it was gone. Devin was once again his usual quiet polite self. "I was merely going to make certain I hadn't harmed him," he said, frowning impatiently at Colin as if there was no basis for the threat in Colin's voice.

But Colin hadn't bought the sudden act of innocence. "I'll check on the puppy," he said.

Joe showed up about then. As the man entered the pen, Devin suddenly looked as if he might cry. "When Colin and I came in here, that little puppy," he said, pointing to the runt Colin was now holding, "ran up and nipped my ankle. I was so surprised I jerked my foot and accidently kicked him."

Colin could tell Joe believed Devin. *I'd even have believed him if I hadn't been here to see what really happened,* Colin admitted to himself. "Looked more like a deliberate kick to me," Colin said.

Joe looked stunned.

Devin's chin trembled. "That's a cruel thing to say," he accused, his voice quivering.

Joe placed an arm around Devin's shoulders. "I'm sure it was just an accident. Colin's just very attached to these pups, and he doesn't like to see any of them harmed." After giving Devin a fatherly pat on the shoulder, Joe approached Colin and took the pup. He made a quick examination, then smiled. "And no harm was done," he announced, setting the little dog on the ground. Immediately it scurried to the side of one of its bigger brothers.

Devin looked honestly relieved. The threat of tears disappeared and he smiled lovingly at the runt and his bigger brother. "They look so cute together, I'd hate to break them up," he said. "I'll take both of them."

But Colin had been unnerved by Devin's behavior. He didn't trust him. "No. I want the little one," he said. His gaze leveled on Joe. "You said I could have any one of the litter I wanted."

"I did." Joe turned toward Devin with apology on his face. "I'm afraid the little one is spoken for."

Devin frowned in disappointment. "I'll pay you extra."

Joe shook his head. "I'm a man of my word," he replied. Then, also being a businessman, he added, "Besides, you want the best for your dad. That runt may be cute, but he'll never take any prizes at a show. He's too small."

"I suppose you're right and I'd only planned on buying one dog. I'm not sure my father would have room for two," Devin conceded and then proceeded to allow Joe to chose the best of the litter for him.

Holding the runt, Colin had felt sure he'd saved the dog's life.

Or maybe I overreacted, and now I want to remember the incident that way because I want to believe that Devin

Smythe isn't quite as nice as most people in this town think he is, he admitted to himself. Abruptly he shoved this childhood memory to the back of his mind and returned his attention to the present. Grudgingly he acknowledged that the adult Devin Smythe was not only wealthy and personable, with a quiet reserved manner, but he had grown into a strikingly handsome man—a perfect catch for any woman. And, Madaline MacGreggor had been the lucky bride. Colin's hand balled into a white-knuckled fist as he fought to ignore a sudden jab of pain deep inside. Damn! he cursed silently, furious that she could still cause him to experience a surge of jealousy. *You're a fool, Colin Darnell,* he chided himself.

Aloud he said coolly, "I'm sure you'll make this job a success." He'd been so certain that one encounter with her would rid him of his demons. But instead, the memory of how good she had felt in his arms was coming back sharp and strong. He wanted out of there and fast. "As long as you've made the changes I requested, you can consider the plans approved. Go ahead and have the men get started clearing the land. I'll depend on you to double-check the stakes once the survey team has come in and set them." He nodded toward the blueprints. "Is my set ready?"

Madaline's movements felt stilted and clumsy to her as she picked up the cardboard tube lying on her desk. "These are yours," she said, and marveled that she could speak coherently and actually sound in control. Their hands remained a good foot apart as he accepted the container, even so she was acutely aware of his nearness. A surge of heat spread through her. But then, he'd always had a very physical effect on her, she recalled.

Colin hadn't thought being close to her could cause such a strong reaction. Now he realized how wrong he'd been. The urge to draw her into his arms, to feel her against him, was close to overwhelming. He had to get out of there.

"Thanks," he said, already moving toward the door. "Have a good day, Mrs. Smythe," he added over his shoulder as he opened it and walked out. This last was more for him than her. He needed to address her by her married name. It helped remind him that she'd chosen to marry another man.

"I apologize for Colin," Richard said, reminding Madaline of his presence. He'd remained where he had been standing when Colin had entered. There was concern on his face. "I didn't realize you two knew one another."

"It was several years ago," Madaline replied, her gaze still on the open door Colin had just walked through. She heard his footsteps come to a halt just beyond her view and guessed he was waiting for the lawyer to join him. In a voice loud enough to carry into the anteroom, she added dryly, "And there is no need for you to apologize. He's always been a difficult man to get along with."

Richard gave her a reassuring smile. "I'm sure you'll be a match for him." Then, adding a quick goodbye, he left her office.

As the outside door closed behind the men, Samantha rose from her desk and stood in the doorway of Madaline's office. There was a dubious expression on her face. "Wasn't that Colin Darnell?" she asked, glancing over her shoulder as if afraid he might suddenly come back and hear her.

"Yes," Madaline replied.

"I never expected to see him back in town," Samantha continued, still looking toward the door. "I remember him as being the strong silent type, but I don't think I've ever seen anyone so grim." Her gaze shifted back to Madaline, and interest shone in her eyes. "You dated him once, didn't you?"

"That was a long time ago," Madaline said, her voice carrying the message that this subject was not open to discussion.

Samantha again glanced toward the door. "What was he doing here?"

"He's my client," Madaline replied, still finding this turn of events difficult to accept.

Samantha's attention jerked back to her employer. "Your client?" She gave her shoulders a shake. "He unnerves me."

Madaline smiled wryly. "He can have that effect on people," she replied, recalling her first real encounter with Colin. She'd been twelve at the time. He'd been sixteen. Her father had hired Colin's father to put a new roof on their home, and Colin was helping. A couple of days earlier, Harvey Clark had tossed her favorite stuffed animal up onto the lower portion of the roof. Harvey, she mused, remembering the big, brown-haired boy who had lived next door. He'd been a year older than she and was her childhood nemesis, but in the end Harvey had turned out to be his own worst enemy. He was dead now. About four years ago, he'd been driving under the influence of drugs and alcohol and crashed into a tree. However, when Madaline was twelve, he derived his pleasure from tormenting her. Her father had a bad back and hadn't been able to climb up and retrieve her stuffed toy.

When Colin and his father had arrived, she'd thought about asking one of them to get the animal for her, but she'd felt intimidated by Colin's presence. So instead, she'd bided her time. They'd had another job to finish before they could start on the roof. As a result, by the time they'd unloaded their ladders and other supplies, it was noon.

She waited until they left for lunch, then went around the house. To her delight, they'd left one of the ladders leaning against the house. She made her way to the roof and climbed out onto it. But the moment she was free from the ladder, she panicked. The roof felt slippery and she was terrified that if she moved she would fall. She also wasn't certain how to get back on the ladder without knocking it over. So there she was, trapped on the roof on her hands and knees. The vision of Colin Darnell being the one to find her like that glowed vividly in her mind, and a rush of embarrassment swept through her.

"I knew it," a male voice suddenly sounded from behind her.

It was like a nightmare come true, she thought as she looked over her shoulder to see Colin standing on the ladder, scowling at her. "I thought you'd gone home for lunch," she blurted.

"I had," he replied, regarding her coldly. "Then ran all the way back here," he added, the red flush on his face giving proof to his words. "I just knew you'd gone and gotten yourself in trouble."

"I'm not in trouble," she lied.

Impatience flickered in his eyes. "You want to tell me what you're doing on this roof?"

Telling him about the stuffed animal suddenly seemed much too childish. "I came up to see what the view was like," she replied.

"Well, you've seen it," he returned. "Now get down from there before you fall and break your neck."

Her cheeks went scarlet. "I'm not sure how to."

"I knew it," he muttered again under his breath, a tinge of amazement in his voice as if he was shocked by how right he'd been. Then with an impatient snort, he said, "I'll get you down."

Following his instructions, she managed to get onto the ladder. Then he quickly climbed to the ground and held it steady so she could descend. As soon as she was down, he lifted the ladder away from the house and laid it on the ground. Turning to her, he said with terse reprimand, "Do you think you can stay out of trouble so that I can go eat my lunch?"

She'd been going to thank him, but the way he made it sound as if she was a nuisance he'd suddenly been cursed with, rankled her. Unable to think of anything snappy to reply, she tossed him a haughty glance and stalked off.

Later that afternoon she was sitting on the front porch when he came around the house carrying the small cloth cat. "You lose this?" he asked, an amused gleam in his eyes.

He made her feel five years old rather than twelve. "It belongs to the neighbor's baby," she lied. "I just wanted to return it."

He smiled an indulgent smile as if to say he'd seen through her ploy but was too mature to tease her. "Here it is, then," he said and tossed it to her.

She'd seen the grin on his face when he turned away to go back around the house. Anger had filled her and she'd assured herself that she'd be happy if he never crossed her path again. *And that would have been for the best,* she added.

"Well, if you ask me, I think you should reconsider accepting his contract," Samantha advised, bringing Madaline's mind back to the present.

"I am," Madaline admitted.

"When you asked me to act as your go-between on this deal, you never mentioned you knew Madaline MacGreggor-Smythe personally," Richard said, glancing over at Colin as he drove them back to the small airport in the next town.

"I didn't think it was important," Colin replied.

"We've been friends for a number of years now. I thought you trusted me. Do you want to tell me the real reason you've come back here?" Richard prodded.

Colin's jaw tensed. "To put the past behind me."

Richard shook his head. "Seems to me this is more like opening an old wound. Maybe you should reconsider."

"Maybe I should," Colin agreed.

A little later, as he sat in the chartered plane winging its way back to Boston, he told himself again he was crazy even to have set foot in Smytheshire again. He'd built a good life in Boston. He had his own construction company, specializing in home improvement. Although new construction was slow, he had more job offers than he could accept. Part of his success was due to the fact that his company did quality work. Another part had been luck. One of the first jobs he'd contracted for after reaching Boston had been for one of the wealthier, influential families of Boston. They'd liked his work and recommended him to all their friends.

He should be happy with the life he had, he told himself again. He couldn't change the past. Maggie had made her choice. He'd never intended to see her again. It was that damn letter! he cursed mentally. He'd read it so many times he had it memorized. Of course it had only been a few words:

> If you still think of Madaline MacGreggor as a friend, she needs your help.

There was no signature. The postmark on the envelope had been Griswoldville, a town not far from Smytheshire.

Colin closed his eyes. Maggie's image, the way she had looked that morning, all cool and businesslike, entered his mind. She didn't seem like a woman who needed anyone's help. The note was probably a practical joke, he decided.

A grimness descended over his features. Continuing the plans for the house on Sanctuary Ridge was a fool's game, and he'd never been one to play the fool—at least not intentionally.

Chapter Two

"You look troubled."

Madaline was sitting on the brocade-covered sofa toward the west end of the large, elegantly furnished living room of Devin Smythe's spacious mansion. She was staring broodingly off into space. Devin's mansion—that was how she thought of this place. Even after two years of living here, she still didn't think of it as her home.

She did have to admit that life here was luxurious. Devin had a staff of five to take care of their every need. There were four day employees—two maids and two gardeners. Then there were two live-in servants. One was Claire Rochel, Devin's cook. She was in her late fifties, widowed with two married children who still lived in town. The second was Mrs. Grayson, the housekeeper. She was a kind motherly woman in her early fifties. Both she and her husband had come here to work when Devin had first moved into the place. Mr. Grayson, who had been in charge of overseeing the greenhouses and gardens, had died of a heart attack several years earlier. Charles Henley was head gardener now. But he didn't live on the estate. He had a house in town.

Thus Mrs. Grayson and Claire were the sole occupants of the servant's wing. *This house is more of a home to the two of them than it is to me,* Madaline mused. She felt like a visitor on an extended stay. *Which is exactly what I am,* she reminded herself dryly. Pushing these thoughts aside, she turned and smiled at the man who had just joined her.

Devin was only four years her senior, but there was a dignity in his carriage and a maturity in his manner that made him seem much older. She noticed that his conservatively styled blond hair had a sheen of moisture and guessed he'd just come from working in his greenhouses. A smudge of black soil on his khaki slacks provided proof that this assumption was correct. As her gaze returned to his classically handsome face, it occurred to her that his physique was classic, too. Thanks to his daily workouts in his private gym, his six-foot frame was as muscular as any Michelangelo statue. She felt a nudge of guilt when she saw the concern in his blue eyes. She hated causing him even a moment's worry. She'd planned to put on a cheerful facade for him, but that probably wouldn't have fooled him, anyway. Devin knew her better than anyone did. She'd never been able to hide anything from him.

"It has been an unusual day," she confessed.

"Tell me about it," he coaxed, seating himself in the velvet upholstered wing chair across from her.

Madaline slipped off her shoes. The urge to put her feet up on the coffee table in front of her was strong. In the modest middle-class home she'd grown up in, that would have been acceptable. But here in Devin's house, everything was so exquisite. She felt as if she had to treat his belongings as if they were museum pieces. In truth, several were. She slipped her feet back into her shoes. Her smile faded as she met his gaze levelly.

"Colin Darnell is back in town."

Interest mingled with the concern in his eyes. "I never thought we'd see him again. After he left town, he didn't even come back to visit his parents. And now that Troy Darnell has retired and he and his wife have moved to Florida, I thought all Colin's ties here were severed."

"I thought so, too." Madaline's gaze shifted to the antique porcelain figurine on the table near the window. But her eyes didn't focus on it. Instead, the piece of porcelain remained a blur as the way Colin had looked standing in her office filled her mind. "I don't understand why he's come back," she said, voicing the thought that had been nagging at her since that morning.

"Has he been bothering you?"

The protectiveness in Devin's voice caused her to turn back toward him. He'd been so good to her. Again she felt a wave of guilt for causing him even a moment's worry. "He's not exactly bothering me," she replied. "He's my client." Even as she said these words, she had to admit that she was still finding this turn of events difficult to adjust to. It seemed more like a bad dream.

Devin frowned skeptically. "Do you think that's wise?"

She'd known he was going to ask her that. And if she was to answer him honestly, she knew she'd have to say that it *wasn't* wise. But pride refused to allow her to admit that Colin could still affect her. Instead, a cool edge entered her voice.

"It seems I've been working for him for a while. He's the one who bought Zebulon's land and is building the house on Sa—" She stopped herself. Not even Devin knew that she and Colin had named that ridge. "The house above the lake," she finished.

The frown on Devin's face deepened. "I thought a Boston lawyer had contracted you for that."

Her jaw tensed. "I thought so, too. But today I learned he was acting for Colin."

An expression of disapproval spread over Devin's features. "I've never liked to be critical of my fellow man. We've all got our shortcomings. But Colin does seem to have a strong bent for deceit."

"Yes, it would seem he does," she agreed grimly, as painful memories assailed her. It angered her that after all this time the hurt and disillusionment was still so intense.

"I'm sure we can find some way to break the contract," Devin said.

All day Madaline had been holding a debate with herself. Abruptly she reached a decision. "No." She met Devin's gaze levelly. "Maybe this is for the best. I thought I had put the past behind me, but lately old memories have been haunting me. It's time I exorcised them and got on with my life."

Leaning forward, Devin took her hands in his. "I don't want to see you hurt again," he said. "Maybe you should reconsider."

Devin could be persuasive, and she'd grown into the habit of following his advice. *Because it's been good advice,* she reminded herself. If she'd followed it four years ago, she wouldn't have been hurt by Colin Darnell. But she refused to allow Colin to think she was afraid of him. "I'm older and I'm wiser." Determination glistened in her eyes. "No man will ever make a fool of me again, especially Colin Darnell."

For a moment Devin looked displeased. Then his expression relaxed and he gave her hands a reassuring squeeze. "Jut remember I'm always here if you need someone to lean on."

"You're my best friend," she admitted with gratitude. "And you've always been the one person I could count on." Then her shoulders stiffened and her face took on an expression of resolve. "But I don't want you to worry. I can handle this on my own. It's something I have to do."

"All right," he conceded. "But promise me you'll give a yell if you find you need a helping hand."

She knew Devin was concerned only for her welfare, but a wave of irritation at his overprotectiveness washed over her. *He's acting as if I'm still a silly child,* she thought. In the next instant, she berated herself. When she was still in grade school, Devin had chosen the role of her guardian angel and she'd allowed him to play it. It wasn't fair for her to be angry with him now. "I promise."

Devin smiled with relief. "And now I think it's time for us to prepare for dinner," he said, releasing her hands and rising. "You know how fussy Claire is about serving her food on time." He breathed an indulgent sigh. "If she wasn't such a good cook, I'd have fired her long ago."

"She's been cooking for your family since before you were born," Madaline pointed out with an indulgent look of her own. "You know you could never fire her, no matter how many tantrums she threw."

"You're right," Devin conceded with a laugh as she rose and he followed her out of the room.

But it wasn't just Claire's long sojourn with the family that ensured her position in Devin's home, Madaline mused climbing the wide winding staircase to the second floor. Devin was fond of the woman, and he was willing to forgive nearly any imperfections in people he cared about. As a general rule he was kind to everyone. Admittedly there were a few people he didn't particularly like, but even to those he exhibited a polite tolerance. There had only been one instance she'd ever known of when he'd been so angry with someone he'd refused to forgive him. She shrugged off that memory. It had been a silly incident and totally out of character for Devin. The fact that she'd never seen a repeat of it assured her that it had been an aberration.

"See you in a few minutes," she said over her shoulder as she reached her bedroom and entered.

Inside, she went to the closet and took out a pale green silk dress. It was Devin's favorite, and she felt as if she owed him some special consideration tonight. She was still feeling guilty for having caused him any worry. And, she admitted grudgingly, she was still feeling guilty for being angered by his protectiveness. That had been totally unfair.

As she quickly dressed, she breathed a tired sigh. Just once she would have liked to go down to dinner in jeans and an old sweatshirt. But Devin liked to dress formally for the evening meal. It was a tradition he had been raised with. Conceding to this wish was small payment for all he'd done for her.

A defensiveness suddenly entered her eyes. "Of course, my being here as his wife has benefited him, too. Without me, he wouldn't be getting his inheritance," she murmured. It shook her that she suddenly found herself feeling as if she had to defend her position in Devin's home.

She frowned at her image in the mirror. Well, she wouldn't be here that much longer, anyway. When Devin had suggested the marriage, he'd also made it clear that he wanted her to remain in his home as his wife only for as long as she wanted. And she had been firm about their getting a divorce fairly soon after he had his inheritance.

"I want a real life," she said, admitting for the first time that she felt as if she had been living in limbo for the past few years. Colin Darnell abruptly entered her mind. "No." The word came out firmly as she vanquished his image. But down deep inside a frustration lingered.

A headache began to build at her temples. Closing her eyes, she rubbed the back of her neck. "This has been a very difficult day," she muttered. Unable to stop herself, she played back the events.

Her eyes opened abruptly and an anxious expression spread over her face. She'd been so distracted by Colin's reappearance, she'd almost forgotten the warning regarding her virginity. Should she mention it to Devin?

She hated to add to his worries. All these years he'd kept his impotency a secret, even from his own family. In fact, she was the only person, other than his doctor, who knew. "And I can't believe anyone could guess the truth," she reasoned aloud. Even the servants were convinced that she and Devin had consummated their marriage. Everyone simply assumed that she and he occupied separate bedrooms because he suffered from periods of insomnia and didn't want to continually disturb her sleep.

"There's no real reason to tell him about the caller," she assured the image in the mirror. "The threat wasn't directed at him. In fact, the more I think about it, the more certain I am that it had to have been a practical joke." She scowled reprovingly. "A very *bad* practical joke."

She gave her shoulders a shake. "And I've been talking to myself much too much lately." A sense of isolation swept through her. "But then, I don't have anyone else to talk to." Until this moment, it had not dawned on her how far she had drifted away from all of her other friends. She'd been so busy with her career and what spare time she had was occupied by Devin that now he was truly the only person in whom she felt comfortable confiding. But she hadn't even been able to talk to him about why Sanctuary Ridge or the plans for the house she was designing were bothering her. She hadn't wanted to admit, even to herself, that her memories from the past could still affect her so strongly.

Her jaw tensed. "However, I intend to use this opportunity to put them to rest."

The tinkling of a bell from downstairs brought a halt to her private conversation. Quickly slipping on her shoes, she hurried out of her room.

While Madaline ate dinner and determinedly kept the conversation between her and Devin focused on the new greenhouse he wanted her to design for him, Colin paced the floor of his living room. Seeing Maggie again had been much more difficult than he'd expected.

When he'd first received the letter suggesting she was in need of some sort of help, he'd wanted to ignore it. After all, she'd cut him out of her life swiftly and cleanly, without even a backward glance. But he hadn't been able to forget about the letter.

The truth was he had never completely gotten Maggie out of his mind. Even after all this time, there was a lingering anger that continued to eat at him. But along with that anger was concern. He knew Maggie had suffered a lot of tragedy these past four years. A month after she had graduated from college, her father had died in a car crash. Colin had learned about the death from his mother the night before the funeral. He'd meant to stay away, but the next day he'd driven back to Smytheshire. No one had seen him, though. As he drove toward the church, he'd glimpsed Maggie and her mother being helped up the steps by Devin. Calling himself a fool for thinking that Maggie might need him, he'd kept on driving. Soon after the funeral, her mother had been diagnosed with cancer. The doctors had performed surgery and Molly MacGreggor had undergone chemotherapy, but neither had done any good and she'd died a year later. It was during that year that Maggie had married Devin.

When Colin learned about the marriage, he'd been determined to put her out of his mind. And he'd convinced himself he had—until the letter arrived. For the next couple of days after receiving it, he'd been a tyrant to be around. Finally, admitting to himself that he needed to put the past to rest, and to do that he was going to have to become involved in Maggie's life again, he started making plans to build the house on Sanctuary Ridge. Admittedly the building of a house was a fairly big undertaking. But ever since he'd been fourteen and first seen the ridge, he'd envisioned having a home there. And once he had Maggie out of his system, he'd enjoy having a retreat in the mountains to escape to once in a while, he'd told himself.

But now, tonight, he was questioning the wisdom of his actions. He'd expected the anger that seeing her again had stirred up in him. What he hadn't expected was to feel the same physical attraction to her he used to feel—and just as strongly as when he'd believed she loved him.

"She's a married woman and she never honestly cared for me in the first place," Colin growled at himself.

And she hadn't looked like a woman who needed anyone's help, he thought for the umpteenth time. Besides, she had Devin to look after her. Something that felt very much like jealousy jabbed sharply at his insides again. His jaw tensed. Devin was welcome to her. Decisiveness etched itself into his features. He reached for the phone. He'd call her and tell her he'd changed his mind about building the house. Then he'd burn the blueprints and the letter, return the deed to the land to Zebulon Lansky and forget about Maggie and Smytheshire forever.

But his hand stopped before it reached the receiver. Grimly, he realized that Maggie was the reason he'd never married. During the past four years, he'd spent a great deal of energy denying she still had any effect on him, but he could deny it no longer. He needed to get her out of his system once and for all. Trying to forget her hadn't worked. Seeing her, getting to know the real Madaline MacGreggor—the cold, calculating woman who lurked just below the surface of what he had thought was a gentle, loving female—was the only way.

Chapter Three

Early in the morning a week later, Maggie stood on the edge of Sanctuary Ridge. A hundred feet below her was Lanksy Lake, its crystal-blue waters reflecting the rays of the early-morning sun. Half of its perimeter was surrounded by hilly forested land. Along the other half was the semicircle of cliffs that formed the ridge. For as far as the eye could see, nature ruled. That was the way old Zebulon liked it. He'd allowed the major portion of his land to remain wild.

When she'd been informed that he'd sold the forty-eight acres on the east side of his property that included the ridge, she'd been surprised. Zebulon was so old he'd outlived all of his immediate family and most of his distant relatives, as well. His land was all he had left of what he loved, and he guarded it zealously. But now that she knew who the buyer was, she understood. Zebulon had liked Colin, probably because Colin was one of the few people in Smytheshire who wasn't afraid of the old man.

She drew a shaky breath. When she was younger, she'd been terrified of Zebulon. Even then he'd seemed ancient, his tall lean frame slightly stooped with age and his white hair hanging long and shaggy, well past his shoulders. A full beard and mustache obscured his face. The only truly discernible features were his blue eyes that studied the world coldly and warned people to keep their distance. He always wore a red plaid shirt and blue jeans with heavy hunting boots that laced up to his knees. No one was quite sure how old he was. Some said he was over a hundred. She was certain he was well into his nineties. And, she confessed, he still unnerved her.

A breeze stirred her hair. It was April, but in the mountains there was still the chill of winter in the air. She took a few steps back from the edge of the ridge. As she seated herself on a nearby boulder, her mind wandered back to the first time she'd come up here. She'd been twenty-one, and it had been June. An unusually hot humid June, she recalled, almost able to feel the sweat that had trickled down her cheek as she'd made the climb through the woods to this spot. She'd been terrified of being discovered by the old man, but that day she'd refused to allow fear to stop her.

Her reason for being there had begun the night before. She and a couple of girlfriends had gone to the small movie theater Marshall Rice had been operating for years. The business barely paid for itself, but Marshall liked movies and since he was retired, he said running the place gave him something to do and he didn't need to make a real income from it. With very little else for entertainment in their rural community, the theater was the Saturday night hangout for the teenagers and young adults. When Madaline and her friends left after the show, Harvey Clark was loitering around outside.

"You two shoo," he ordered, flicking his hand at her two friends. "I'm going to walk Madaline home. It's on my way."

His eyes had a glassy look, and as his breath wafted past her, Madaline smelled liquor. But even if he'd been sober, she wouldn't have agreed to allow him to walk her home. She didn't trust Harvey. "I don't want your company," she informed him and, hooking arms with her friends she walked away with them.

A couple of blocks later, she parted company with her friends. They'd offered to walk her all the way to her door, but they lived on a different street and she didn't want to inconvenience them. Besides, Smytheshire was a peaceful, quiet town, the kind where everyone knew everyone else. She'd walked home alone after dark many nights and never worried. Harvey's manner had left her a little nervous, but she had only half a block to go on her own. "I'll be fine," she assured them.

But as she passed Harvey's house, he suddenly stepped out from behind a large growth of shrubbery and blocked her path. "You weren't very nice to me back there," he said, his speech slurred, providing even more evidence that he'd been drinking.

She was used to his pestering her. Normally, she just found it irritating, but tonight his drunkenness made her uneasy. "Leave me alone," she ordered. Attempting to keep a distance between them, she began to walk around him.

Reaching out, he caught her by the arm. "Now don't rush off."

Anger swept through Madaline. She was sick and tired of Harvey making her life uncomfortable. "Let go of me!" she demanded, trying to jerk her arm free and at the same time kicking him in the leg.

Fury brought a deep flush to his face. "You little . . . !" he growled, his hand moving into striking position.

Her bid for freedom had failed and his hold on her arm had tightened painfully. She threw her other arm up and ducked in an attempt to avoid the coming blow.

But the blow was never delivered. "It's not polite to strike a female," a familiar male voice said in a threatening tone.

Madaline looked up as Colin Darnell caught Harvey by the wrist. Shock raced through her as she realized she wasn't surprised to see him. It was as if she had known he would come to rescue her. *That's ridiculous,* she chided herself. She'd simply been hoping that someone would come along.

Both of the men were the same age, but Harvey had a couple of inches on Colin and about fifty more pounds. Harvey's bulk was mostly flab, though, and Colin's was muscle. When Harvey tried to yank his wrist from Colin's grasp, Colin held it easily. But Madaline knew that Harvey had a belligerent streak that verged on stupidity. She glanced toward Colin anxiously.

"This ain't none of your business, Darnell," Harvey snorted. "Go away."

"Everyone in town is getting fed up with your bullying," Colin replied, his voice level and cold. "I'm warning you to stop it. And to begin with, you're going to apologize to Madaline and then you're going to leave her alone."

For a moment Harvey looked as if he was going to argue, then a sheepish grin spread over his face. "Sure," he agreed.

Madaline had seen that look before. She was about to warn Colin not to trust Harvey, but before she could get the words out, Harvey had released her and taken a swing at Colin. The punch landed on Colin's nose.

"Damn!" Colin growled.

An instant later Harvey was lying flat on his back, clutching his stomach with one hand and his bleeding nose with the other. "I'm going to get you for this, Darnell," he ground out through clenched teeth. Then, getting to his feet, he stumbled toward his house.

"Are you all right?" Colin asked, turning toward Madaline.

"I'm fine. Thank..." Her words of gratitude died on her lips. With only the moonlight to illuminate the night, his features were shadowed, but she could still see he was bleeding. "Your nose," she said with concern.

His hand followed the direction of her gaze. He grimaced with pain when it reached the fast-swelling area at the bridge of his nose.

Madaline quickly retrieved a packet of tissues from her purse and handed it to him, regarding him anxiously. "I'm so sorry," she said.

"It's nothing," he replied, holding the tissues so that they would stop the flow of blood.

Her gaze shifted and suddenly she was looking into those dark eyes of his. Even shadowed by the night, they seemed to glimmer with an inner fire. A warm tingling sensation began in the tips of her toes and traveled through her. The urge to move closer to him was so strong she almost took a step forward. But shyness held her back.

"You look pretty shaken," he said gruffly.

Stop gaping at him, she ordered herself. *He'll think you're addled.* "You're the one you should be worried about," she replied. "Come on up to the house. I think we better put some ice or something on your nose." Her anxiety increased. "Maybe we should call Dr. James."

"It's just a bloody nose." He squared his shoulders as if to indicate that this was nothing to concern herself about. "But I'll walk you to your door to be sure Harvey leaves you alone."

He'd already started toward her house. Silently she fell into step beside him. But as they neared her front door and she could see his face more clearly in the light from the porch lamp, her stomach knotted. His nose was not only swelling, it was also a painful shade of red. "Please, come in and let my mom take a look at it," she pleaded.

"I'll go home and put some ice on it," he replied, his tone letting her know it was useless for her to argue with him.

It's obvious he wants to get away from me as quickly as possible, she thought ruefully. "Thank you again," she said, and went inside.

She'd meant to go straight upstairs, but instead she found herself stopping to watch him from the window by the door as he walked away. He was wearing clean but well-worn jeans, a T-shirt and sneakers. His usual attire, she thought, then frowned at herself. He never paid any attention to her and she didn't like admitting that she paid enough attention to him to know what he normally wore. But not to admit it would be a lie. She'd found herself noticing him a great deal through the years. But then in a town this small, she reasoned, it was only natural to be aware of other townsfolk. Grudgingly she also admitted that she'd known the moment he walked into the movie theater that night. And she'd experienced a twinge of pleasure that he hadn't had a date. Instead, he'd been with a group of his buddies. However, she reminded herself, he'd never shown any interest in her or even given her a second glance. Mentally she cringed as she recalled the look of superior adulthood on his face the day he'd presented her with her stuffed animal.

"And I don't know why I'm even giving him a second thought," she muttered to herself as he disappeared from her view.

But later that night, the tingling sensation she'd experienced when she'd been standing alone with him taunted her.

The next morning, she'd awakened with Colin on her mind. "I'm just anxious about him because he was injured defending me," she told herself.

To her relief it was Sunday. She would see him in church, assure herself that he was fine and then put him out of her mind. But he wasn't in church. His parents were there and, she noted, they didn't look upset or worried. Still, all during the service, she couldn't stop thinking about him.

Later, as she sat eating Sunday dinner with her parents, she had a hard time concentrating on the conversation. Finally, she admitted to herself that she wouldn't feel comfortable until she'd seen for herself that Colin was all right.

After helping her mother with the dishes, she changed into shorts and a lightweight cotton shirt, told her parents she was going for a bike ride and left.

Colin lived in a two-story frame house on the west side of town. She'd once heard his dad say that this home was his best advertisement, and she had to concede that the Darnells' house always looked well cared for. And, thanks to Mrs. Darnell's green thumb, the gardens in front were filled all summer with profusely blooming flowers.

Madaline nervously knocked on the front door. She couldn't stop worrying that the Darnells might blame her for Colin's injury. Though they hadn't cast any angry glances her way during church, the urge to turn and run was strong. But she stood her ground.

"Madaline MacGreggor, isn't it?" Mrs. Darnell said in a friendly voice when she came to the door. "What can I do for you?"

The curiosity in the woman's eyes caused Madaline to guess that Colin had not told his parents the truth about how he'd gotten his bloody nose. Maybe the swelling had gone down and it wasn't even noticeable, she thought. "I was wondering if Colin was home," she said, attempting to keep her tone light and mildly indifferent.

"No, I'm afraid not," Mrs. Darnell replied.

It was faint, but Madaline was sure she saw a flicker of concern in the woman's eyes. "I sort of need to talk to him," she said hesitantly. She didn't want to seem persistent, but after seeing the worry in Mrs. Darnell's eyes, she couldn't simply walk away.

"He's probably out at old Zebulon Lanksy's place," Mrs. Darnell said apologetically.

"Zebulon Lansky's place?" Madaline repeated, sure she had heard the woman wrong. It was common knowledge that Zebulon lived liked a hermit and couldn't abide visitors.

Mrs. Darnell smiled. "Colin does repairs for him once in a while. In payment, Zebulon gives him free run of the land." An indulgent expression played across her face. "'Course that free access doesn't include anyone else." She shook her head. "Never knew anyone to be as private as old Zebulon. Anyway, Colin tells me there's a lake out there with a high cliff on one side. When he wants to be alone, he likes to go out there and hike to the top of the cliff. He says he can see for miles." She smiled once again, and Madaline saw the curiosity return to her eyes. "When he gets home, I'll tell him you were looking for him."

"Thanks," Madaline replied.

As she walked back to where her bike was parked by the white picket gate, she told herself to forget about Colin

Darnell. If he'd been seriously hurt, he'd have been home or in the hospital. "You're making a mountain out of a molehill," she scolded herself.

But when she got on her bike and began peddling away, the direction she took was out of town. "This is crazy," she muttered under her breath a little later as she turned off the main road and started down an old dirt road that skirted the Lanksy property. In the first place, just the thought of trespassing on old Zebulon's land caused her stomach to knot with fear. And in the second place, even if she got up enough nerve to do it, she had no idea where the lake was. "Go home!" she ordered herself.

But before she could act on this command, she saw a blue pickup truck parked by the side of the road. She knew it belong to Colin. She'd seen him driving it. As added proof, the words "Darnell Construction" were painted in white on the doors.

Nearby was a stile over the fence, giving access to the property. It looked fairly new, and she guessed Colin had built it. "Well, he'll be coming back this way," she reasoned aloud as she parked her bike beside the stile. Deciding that sitting on top of the steps that spanned the fence would not mean she was trespassing, she climbed the stile and seated herself.

The woods came all the way to the fence. There did seem to be a rough path leading into them, but common sense told her to wait.

Besides, it was comfortable on her perch. The day was scorching hot. Her long ride had left her tired and soaked with sweat. Here on the stile she was in the shade, and there was even a light breeze. "A nice cold drink would be pleasant, too," she mused, wishing she'd had the presence of mind to bring some water along.

She wasn't certain how long she'd been sitting there. It felt like forever, but she guessed it had been about half an hour when a dog suddenly came racing out of the woods. He ran to the base of the stile and stood there barking at her. Suddenly her heart began to pound with fear. Following the dog was Zebulon himself. Quickly she swung her legs to the road side of the stile.

"You resting or waiting for Colin?" the old man asked, studying her skeptically.

Her shoulders squared. She refused to let him know how much he frightened her. "Waiting for Colin," she replied.

For a moment he studied her in silence. Then he waved her toward him. "Come on. I might as well take you to him."

For a moment she considered saying she'd prefer to wait. But she realized that Colin might not come back to his truck for hours. *Be brave,* she ordered herself, and swung her legs back over the top of the stile. Then she stopped and looked dubiously down at the dog. The animal was watching her as guardedly as his master.

"He won't bite," Zebulon said. His gaze leveled on the dog. "Come on, mutt," he commanded and the animal hurried off back into the woods.

Still Madaline hesitated.

"Despite any rumors you may have heard to the contrary, I don't bite, either," the old man added.

She saw the amusement in his eyes and knew *he* knew she was afraid. Embarrassed that he obviously thought she was a silly child who would be scared of her own shadow, her back stiffened. Without any further hesitation, she climbed down from the stile and followed him.

He didn't speak once as they wove their way upward. It was a fairly steep incline, and her legs were already tired from the bike ride. About the time she thought they were going to give out from under her, they reached more level land. A couple of minutes later, she and Zebulon emerged into a natural clearing created by a large flat exposed rock formation. They had reached the top of the cliff. Colin was seated on a boulder near the edge looking out at the vast landscape below. He turned toward them, his expression grim.

"Found this female looking for you," Zebulon informed him. "Been my experience that women are nothing but trouble." He suddenly grinned. "Looks like you've already found that out." Without waiting for a response, he called to his dog and headed back out of the clearing.

Madaline stood staring at Colin. His nose was swollen and he had two black eyes. "I'm really sorry," she said shakily, taking a step toward him.

Self-directed anger spread over his face. "It wasn't your fault. I should have been keeping an eye on him."

Madaline took another step forward. Her stomach knotted at the sight of the ugly bruising. "Is your nose broken?" she heard herself ask in a voice barely above a whisper.

He gave a shrug. "Doc says it's just a small fracture." His gaze leveled on her. "What did you want to see me for?"

The note of impatience in his voice made her feel like an intruder. "I just wanted to make sure you were all right." It was obvious she wasn't welcome here and she felt like a fool for coming. "Now that I know you weren't seriously hurt, I'll be on my way."

He was on his feet before she reached the edge of the clearing. "You'll get lost on your own," he said, the impatience in his voice even more evident. "I'd better lead you out. Where'd you park?"

She swung around to face him. "My bike is by the stile. And I can find my way just fine on my own. Sorry I disturbed your afternoon."

He continued toward her. "I'll come along, anyway, just to make certain you get back. Wouldn't want Devin accusing me of letting his girl get lost or hurt."

She scowled at the patronizing tone in his voice. "I'm not going to get lost or hurt. *And* I'm not Devin's girl."

He cocked an eyebrow in a gesture of disbelief. "Seems to me that might be news to him."

"Devin and I are just friends," she retorted. Suddenly the world seemed to start to spin. A wave of nausea swept through her, and the headache she'd been trying to ignore began to throb painfully. Her legs weakened and she felt herself sinking to the ground.

Before she could collapse completely on the rocky surface, two strong arms caught her, and she felt herself being gently lowered into a sitting position. Vaguely she was aware that Colin had sat down beside her. Like a limp doll, she rested against him, her head on his shoulder and his arm around her for support.

"I don't know what happened," she muttered, her mind confused, the headache and nausea making it difficult to concentrate.

"I don't suppose you brought along any water to drink," she heard him say.

"I didn't expect to go for a bike ride in the country or to climb a mountain to find you," she returned gruffly.

"Here, drink this," he ordered.

In the next moment, her head was being lifted away from him. This bothered her. In spite of the headache and dizziness, she'd liked the feel of his solid shoulder against her cheek. *I liked it because it saved me from having to lie on the rough rock,* she told herself as water wet her lips. Suddenly the primitive urges of survival took over, and she began to swallow.

"You got dehydrated," he said with a terse reprimand.

The dizziness faded and her strength began to return. His attitude was getting on her nerves. "You could at least show the same amount of sympathy for me that I've shown for you," she grumbled. "And you could thank me for not throwing up all over you."

A sheepishness came over his features. "Sorry," he replied remorsefully. "Guess I'm not in a very good mood today."

"Are you ever?" she asked dryly, then flushed when she realized what she'd said.

"I have my moments," he replied with equal dryness.

Madaline clamped her mouth shut. She'd already made a big enough fool of herself for one day.

"You feel strong enough to get down the hill?" Colin asked, gently easing her to her feet.

"I think so," she replied, attempting to move away from him.

But his hold on her waist tightened. "I think I'd better help," he said.

She wanted to refuse but knew that it would be stupid. Her legs still felt rubbery.

When they reached his truck, he insisted she climb in. Then, tossing her bike into the back, he drove her home. They didn't talk. She considered saying something to break the uneasy silence between them, but she couldn't think of anything, and Colin clearly had nothing to say to her. Obviously he considered her intrusion a nuisance. As they pulled into her drive, she saw Devin's sports car.

Colin glanced toward her with a "Who did you think you were trying to kid?" look. Then, still without a word, he got out of the cab and lifted her bike down from the back.

By the time he came around to her side of the cab, she'd climbed out on her own. Her legs still felt wobbly, but she wasn't going to let him see that. "Thanks for the ride," she said stiffly.

"Sure," he replied brusquely. His gaze shifted to a point beyond her. "Looks like you won't be needing my help to get to the house." With that, he strode around his truck, climbed in and drove off.

"What were you doing with Colin Darnell?" Devin questioned, coming up behind her, disapproval in his voice.

"Being infuriated," she answered, attempting to ignore her sudden sharp sensation of aloneness.

Devin laughed lightly. "Tell me what happened?"

And she did—well, not everything. She told him the basic facts but chose not to mention the effect Colin had on her. Devin was furious when he heard about Harvey's behavior and sympathetic about Colin's broken nose. "Harvey needed to be taught a lesson," he said when she finished. Then his manner became stern. "And from now on, I don't want you walking around alone after dark." The look of angry concern changed to one of indulgence. "As for Colin, he's always been a bit on the gruff side. You'd probably be better off to stay away from him."

She'd always appreciated Devin's friendship and advice before, but that Sunday it irritated her. She did not, however, allow her feelings to show. Admitting that her emotions seemed to be on a roller coaster, she decided it would be prudent to maintain a level of calm for the rest of the day. That night, lying in bed, she finally realized that Devin made her feel smothered. He was almost always around. It was no wonder Colin Darnell thought she was Devin's girl.

Colin Darnell. The name conjured up his image in her mind. A heat unrelated to the hot June night spread through her as she recalled the feel of his strong arm around her waist. Then she scowled. The impatience in his manner had made it clear he didn't want her company. That's how he'd always behaved toward her. If he'd been with a group of people and she'd stopped to talk to anyone in that group, he'd sort of back away.

That he had been the one to rescue her from Harvey was close to unbelievable. Except, Madaline had to admit in all fairness, Colin had always been one to stand up for what he thought was right, no matter who or what was involved.

"And now that I know he's feeling fine, it's time to put him out of my mind," she told herself.

That was easier said than done. The very next day, she was leaving the post office just as Colin was coming down the street. As usual, Devin was with her. She would have walked past Colin without speaking, but Devin brought them all to a halt.

"Sorry about the black eyes," he said with sympathy. Then he smiled. "They're real beauties."

"Yeah, thanks," Colin replied unenthusiastically. His gaze shifted to Madaline, then to Devin, then back to Madaline. He gave her a look that again called her a liar for saying she wasn't Devin's girl.

Before she could say anything, Devin placed his arm protectively around her shoulders. "I'm grateful to you, Colin," he said, extending his hand.

Mentally Madaline groaned. Devin's action did make it appear as if she was his girl.

She caught the flash of disdain in Colin's eyes as he accepted the handshake. Then, as if he found their company too boring to tolerate a moment longer, he said, "I've got to get to the post office and then back to work." And with that he strode off.

Harvey showed up in town that day sporting a black eye and a swollen jaw. Devin made Madaline promise she wouldn't go anywhere alone. She didn't want to make that promise. Harvey, for the moment at least, was keeping a lot of distance between them, but Devin had been insistent.

As for Colin, Madaline again ordered herself to forget him. But he kept coming back into her mind, and whenever she saw him on the street, a nervousness would invade her. "The only reason Colin Darnell is having this effect on me is because I'm worried that Harvey's going to do something vengeful to him and I'll blame myself," she reasoned, refusing to admit she could honestly care for a man who considered her a pest.

By the end of the week, her nerves were stretched taut. Devin's nearly constant companionship was growing more and more irritating. Actually it wasn't really Devin's company, she admitted late one night a few days after the meeting in front of the post office. It was that she and Colin seemed to be constantly crossing each other's paths these days, and every time they did, she was always with Devin.

"It doesn't matter who I'm with," she chided herself. Colin Darnell wasn't interested in dating her. "I just don't like looking like a liar."

By the next weekend, her nerves were reaching the breaking point. In spite of all her attempts not to think about Colin, he haunted her dreams. She would be helping him escape Harvey's vengeance. When they were finally safe, or sometimes when they weren't, he'd almost kiss her, then pull back and call her Devin's girl. Then Devin would enter the dream to give proof to this accusation.

"It's not Colin Darnell or Devin that has me so upset," she muttered as she dressed on Saturday morning. It was feeling as if she was living under constant guard. "I'm sure Harvey has decided to leave me alone," she informed her image in the mirror. "And today I'm going to have a talk with Devin. He must have better things to do with his time than escort me every time I leave this house."

And she did have a talk with Devin. At first he hadn't wanted to give up his guardianship, but she'd been firm. When she'd told him that his behavior was causing a strain on their friendship, he'd finally backed down. He did insist that she not go out at night alone, but he agreed that during the day, he would not be her shadow....

Her shadow. The words played through Madaline's mind as she sat on the boulder near the cliff edge. She closed her eyes so tightly they hurt as she tried to shut out these images from the past. She knew now that it would have been wiser to allow Devin to remain her shadow. She squeezed her eyes more tightly shut. She didn't want to think about the past. It couldn't be changed. It was best forgotten.

Chapter Four

"So, Colin's really going to build that house up here."

The elderly male voice caused Madaline's eyes to snap open. The memories of the past conjured up by this place faded, as she jerked around and saw Zebulon entering the clearing.

He frowned in confusion as he approached. "Thought you were married to that Smythe boy. You getting a divorce so's you can marry Colin?"

No one could ever accuse Zebulon of being subtle, Madaline thought. But she didn't hold it against him. She preferred bluntness to hedging around a question. "No, I'm not getting a divorce. I'm here because I've been hired to design the house."

Zebulon had stopped a few feet from her. Leaning on his walking stick, he studied her. "My dad and granddad helped found this town with your husband's great-granddad."

There was a curiosity in his eyes that surprised Madaline. As a general rule, Zebulon was indifferent to the other residents of Smytheshire. Even more surprising, he was making casual conversation. That was something he never did. "I know," she replied.

He continued to study her closely. "That husband of yours ever talk about his great-granddad or about the settling of our little community?"

"No," Madaline said, wondering if Zebulon was actually going to reminisce. It was natural for the elderly to recant their past history and that of their forebears, she knew. Maybe Zebulon had finally reached a stage in his life when he felt this need.

Zebulon shrugged. "Guess that would make for boring dinner conversation, especially for a young married couple." Leaning forward on his cane, he brought his face closer to hers. "Never thought much of marriage myself. But I did think you and Colin made a nice couple." He straightened. "'Course there's no telling what goes on in a woman's mind."

Or in a man's, she returned silently. A chill ran down her spine as old memories pushed themselves forward again.

"Oh, come on now, Zebulon," a familiar voice said. "You've always told me women like pretty things and they'll go with a man who can provide them. Seems to me like you know what you're talking about, at least in some cases."

Madaline glanced to her left and saw Colin entering the clearing. She hadn't expected him to return to Smytheshire so soon. She had thought he intended to allow her to oversee the work on the house. But her surprise at his unexpected appearance was only momentary, as she bristled at his blatant insinuation that she'd married Devin for his money. Well, in a way she had, her honest side reminded her. But it hadn't been for herself. A lump of grief formed in her throat. At least she had the satisfaction of knowing that her mother had received the very best medical treatment money could buy.

She faced Colin with cool dignity. "For some of us, a man's moral values are the most important."

Colin scowled at her implication. "There's nothing wrong with my moral values."

"Seems you two have some unfinished personal business to settle," Zebulon said, reminding them of his presence. "I've always made it a point never to get caught in the fray when two wild animals are fighting or when a man and a woman go at one another. So, I'll just be on my way."

"We have no 'personal' business to settle," Madaline said tersely, but Zebulon was already disappearing into the woods.

Colin's attention remained riveted on her. He'd hoped that the strength of her effect on him a week ago had been partially due to his nervousness at seeing her again. But today his reactions were as strong as ever, and the anger he'd felt toward her years ago was just as powerful.

"I'd like to know what right you think you have to question my morals," he demanded.

Madaline turned back toward him. Again a chill of fear shook her. Years ago she hadn't faced him with what she knew about him because it had hurt too much. Now she wasn't certain she had the nerve. He looked even bigger and stronger than he had then and much more dangerous.

Colin was startled by the fear he read in her eyes. He knew he could be overbearing at times, but he'd never thought she was afraid of him. Of course, her reactions to him had always proved to be unpredictable. *And mine toward her were never what anyone would call levelheaded,* he mused dryly, remembering the first time he'd noticed that she'd grown into womanhood. For years he'd thought of her as the little redheaded MacGreggor girl. Then one day, when she was around seventeen, he'd noticed her walking down the street. Her hips had an enticing swing, and the way the sun glinted off her hair brought out its rich burgundy highlights.

"I'd be careful about pursuing that one. Redheads can be a real handful," his father had cautioned with a laugh when he'd noticed the direction his son's attention had taken.

Colin had smiled back self-consciously. He didn't usually allow what he was thinking to show so openly. But then, he'd never experienced such a strong sudden attraction before. "You don't have to worry about me tangling with her," he assured his father. "She's Devin Smythe's girl."

Still, that night, he found himself considering competing with Devin. He knew others had tried. But they'd never been able to hold Madaline's interest. In the end, she'd always gone back to Devin. "And who am I to think I could compete with him and win?" Colin had mocked himself, looking down at his worn work clothes and callused hands. Devin had looks, charm, brains and money. Colin told himself the attraction he'd experienced that afternoon had been merely a fluke, a momentary flash of lust. He'd ordered himself to put her out of his mind.

The next time he saw her was at church on Sunday. He'd assured himself he wouldn't feel anything. But the moment he saw her walking toward him, his muscles tensed and a surge of heat rushed through him. She smiled at something her mother said and he didn't think he'd ever seen a girl look so pretty. He almost went over and talked to her then, but suddenly Devin was by her side, staking his claim.

All that winter and the next summer, he found himself noticing her He tried not to. But telling himself to ignore her was like trying to stop the wind from blowing or the sun from shining. Finally she went away to college. He thought that would be a relief, but it wasn't. It was as if a void had been created in his life. Every weekend, he found himself looking for her to see if she was home for a visit. But when she *was* home, she spent her time with Devin.

That summer Devin and his parents went on an extended tour of Europe and took Madaline with them. It was common knowledge around town that the Smythes were paying all Madaline's expenses. Colin had guessed as much, anyway. He knew her family couldn't afford to send her both to college and to Europe for the summer. There was a bit of gossip, but Mrs. MacGreggor was quick to point out that her daughter was being chaperoned by the Smythes and they could be trusted. No one in town argued with that. They all knew the Smythes were very conservative people. Besides, Madaline and Devin had long ago become a couple in most of the townfolks' minds. It was accepted as inevitable that they would one day wed.

Colin spent that summer, the next year and the following summer attempting to find another woman to hold his interest. But after a couple of dates, he would get bored with his current companion.

Then came the summer before Madaline's last year in college. She had a job at Ed Langley's grocery store, and he and his dad were reroofing several of the buildings on Main Street. Because of that, Colin caught glimpses of her every day. He spent a lot of time telling himself to ignore her, but he wasn't able to heed his own advice.

Then came the night Harvey Clark had gotten drunk. Colin had seen Madaline going into the movie theater with a couple of her girlfriends. He'd joined some friends and gone in, too. All during the movie, he debated whether or not to talk to her afterward. He felt like an idiot. He was twenty-five, a grown man, and this twenty-one-year-old female had him tied in knots. A hundred times he reminded himself that she was Devin's girl, although he was pretty sure she and Devin had no formal commitment to one another. Still, when the movie was finished and everyone exited the theater, he kept his distance. Then he saw Harvey bothering her. He didn't like Harvey and he didn't trust him. Just to be certain she was safe, he decided to follow her to make sure she got home all right. When Harvey came out of the bushes and grabbed her, it pleased Colin greatly to be the one to come to her aid. But he wasn't pleased to get that broken nose. He felt like a fool, and when she came looking for him the next day, he was embarrassed to be seen with his face so black and blue. He couldn't stop thinking of how he'd compared to Devin.

He'd played the fool all round that summer. He hadn't believed her when she'd said she wasn't Devin's girl. But he'd wanted to. He'd wanted to so much, he'd finally asked her for a date. It was a couple of weeks after the incident with Harvey. He and his father were putting a new roof on Paley's Jewelry Store and he saw her walking down the street. He was surprised that Devin wasn't with her. Since Harvey's unwanted advance, Devin had been her constant companion. Colin figured this was his opportunity to prove to himself once and for all that she really was Devin's girl. He'd ask her out, if she refused his invitation, he'd put her out of his mind forever.

He timed his descent down the ladder to coincide with her passing. She was forced to come to a halt when she reached him, because her path was blocked. He'd meant to begin with some sort of small talk, but instead, he said, "If you're really not Devin's girl, how about going out with me this Saturday?"

She looked surprised. Then she'd met his gaze as if accepting a challenge and said, "Sure."

Well, he *had* made it sound like a challenge, he reminded himself. And he'd have been a lot better off if he'd stayed up on that roof that day.

Pushing these memories to the dark recesses of his mind, he studied the woman who now stood in front of him. His jaw tensed and he ran a hand agitatedly through his hair. He'd expected anger or indifference from her. He was prepared for either of those. But the fear he saw in her face shook him.

"Forget I asked," he said brusquely. His manner became businesslike. "Is the survey team on its way?"

Madaline felt dizzy and realized she'd been holding her breath. Slowly she released it. "Yes," she replied, then couldn't stop herself from adding, "I thought you were going to remain in Boston and that I was to oversee the construction of your house."

"I've decided to take a more personal interest in the project," he replied.

Being alone with him was having a disconcerting effect on her. She told herself he was a man she should fear. Yet down deep inside, the memory of his touch was causing a hard knot of longing. She glanced at her watch. It was nearly eight. "The survey team should be arriving any minute," she said, more for her own encouragement than anything else.

Colin heard the relief in her voice and was irritated. "There's no reason for you to be afraid of me, Maggie," he growled. "Mrs. Smythe," he corrected, because she wasn't his "Maggie" anymore. She never had been, not really, he reminded himself.

Madaline hated that her feelings had shown so openly. Pride made her square her shoulders. "I'm not afraid of you." As she made this declaration, she was startled to realize it was more truth than fiction. You *should* be afraid of him, she admonished herself sternly.

Colin was sure she was lying. Her initial reaction of fear had been so obvious. But she'd fooled him once before; he'd thought she was in love with him yet she'd turned away from him and never looked back. "I'm glad to hear that," he said coolly. His gaze narrowed on her. "Because I would never do anything to purposely hurt you or cause you any harm."

Madaline heard the edge of accusation in his voice. If he had added *the way you hurt me,* his point couldn't have been clearer.

Colin jerked his gaze away from her. He was furious with himself. He'd never meant to allow her to guess how deeply her rejection had cut him.

Madaline knew it had been cowardly of her not to face him all those years ago and tell him why she was breaking up with him. Now it was suddenly very important to her that she defend herself to him. "I—" she began.

Colin swung back to face her. "The past is dead," he said, cutting her short. It was too late for explanations, and he sure as hell didn't want to hear her apologizing to him; he had his pride. "I didn't come back here to resurrect it. It's best if we just let it rest."

The hardness in his voice and the coolness of his expression made it clear to Madaline that no matter what she said, he'd never forgive her. She stiffened. She didn't want his forgiveness. Her gaze shifted to the rocky ground at her feet, and the memory that always brought a cold chill of fear played through her mind. Colin Darnell, of all people, had no right to judge her, she told herself curtly.

The sound of voices broke into her thoughts. Glancing toward the woods, she saw four men emerge.

Two of the men were the Kolby brothers, Ray and John. They owned a small local construction company. Both had worked for Colin's dad when they were younger. Mr. Darnell had always spoken highly of them and Madaline knew they did quality work, so she'd hired them for this job. She recognized the third man; he was a surveyor from Greenfield.

"Good to see you again," John said with a smile, approaching Colin and extending his hand. "Your dad taught me most of what I know." The smile remained on his lips, but a worried look entered his eyes. "You planning to come back here and give us some competition?"

Colin smiled reassuringly. "Nope. Just building a place I can escape to when I want to get out of Boston for a while," he replied.

John visibly relaxed and Madaline saw the relief on Ray's face. She couldn't blame them. Jobs were scarce and they didn't need Colin coming back to compete for what work there was.

Ralph Snider, the fourth man in the group, stepped up to Madaline. "I warned John and Ray that you might not take too kindly to them for hiring me," he said. His broad shoulders, strengthened from a life of hard outdoor labor, straightened. As if he suddenly remembered that he was speaking to a woman, Ralph grabbed his hat off his head and held it in his work-callused hands. "But they know I'm a good worker."

Madaline heard the anxiety in his voice and realized he was afraid she might not allow him to work on a project with which she was connected. "I have no problem with you working on this job," she assured him.

The man drew a relieved breath and smiled nervously. "I never meant to upset your husband," he said with apology. "I was just trying to save that old oak. I know how much he values that arboretum he's created. It's a fine piece of work. It just never occurred to me that that mistletoe was one of his experiments. I know I should have asked first. But it's a parasite and been known to kill full-grown trees."

"I know you were only trying to be helpful," Madaline replied. But it had been an upsetting incident, she admitted to herself. It had happened nearly a year ago. She and Devin had been walking in the massive gardens he'd created on the acreage surrounding his house. His plants were the one true love of his life, she thought, as a wave of sympathy for him swept through her. In a way, that justified his loss of temper that day.

Ralph had been working for Devin as head gardener. He'd had the job for nearly five years, and Devin was always praising Ralph's ability with the plants. She and Devin were on their way to the herb garden in the center of a grove of old oaks. He was thinking of putting in some new plantings and wanted her opinion. But as they came into view of the site, Devin had halted abruptly. He'd cursed under his breath, then yelled, "Stop that immediately," and started running toward the largest of the old oak trees.

Startled by this show of temper from a man whom she had rarely heard even raise his voice, Madaline had quickly followed. Ahead, she saw Ralph on a ladder, his shears in his hand.

"I spotted this mistletoe growing on this oak," the gardener said, coming down the ladder as Devin reached him. He was clutching a tangled mass of vines in one hand, a proud smile on his face as if he expected to be thanked. "This stuff has been known to kill oaks bigger and older than this." He gave a knowledgeable nod of his head. "Last night when I went home, I looked it up in one of those horticulture books you gave me."

Devin's face was purple with rage. "You've very possibly ruined an extremely valuable experiment," he snarled.

The smile vanished from Ralph's face. "I was just trying to save the tree."

"You should have asked me before you did anything," Devin returned through clenched teeth.

"Devin, Ralph was only trying to be helpful," Madaline interjected, thoroughly shaken at seeing her husband so close to losing total control of his temper.

Devin took a long deep breath. Then he'd said in a tone that held no compromise, "You're fired. Don't ever set foot on this property again."

Ralph looked as if he was going to protest. Then, with a disgusted scowl, he stalked off. "I was just trying to do my job," Madaline heard him mutter under his breath. "Thought he'd want the tree saved."

"That idiot!" Devin seethed, drawing her attention back to him. She watched him climb the ladder and inspect the branch. "I've been trying to cultivate this species for nearly two years now."

Madaline felt sorry for Ralph, but she knew that Devin's plants were like his children. "Is the plant truly ruined?" she asked sympathetically.

"I think I stopped him in time," Devin replied, coming back down the ladder. He was calmer. "But I've learned a valuable lesson. I shall have a very strong talk with the next head gardener I hire about not doing *anything* to *any* plant until he consults with me."

Madaline had hoped Devin would rehire Ralph. The man had a wife and a family to feed, and he had been a conscientious worker. But Devin hadn't. Instead, he'd hired someone new. She'd never thought of Devin as vindictive or as someone who would hold a grudge, but he was extremely touchy where his plants were concerned. And, she'd reasoned, we all have our faults and petty grievances. Besides, it hadn't been easy living with a paragon. Realizing that Devin had a few imperfections had made her own faults seem less conspicuous.

"I appreciate your open-mindedness," Ralph said, bringing her back to the present. He returned his hat to his head, then rejoined the Kolbys and the surveyor.

Madaline felt a prickling on her neck and turned to see Colin watching her. As the four men began their work, he approached her.

"So, Devin lost his temper over a piece of mistletoe and actually fired a man who had been a faithful employee for years?" He knew it shouldn't matter to him, but it pleased him to point out Devin's unfairness.

"He lost his temper because the plant was part of an experiment he'd been working on," she replied in Devin's defense. Sympathy for Devin filled her. He was a good man who had been treated unjustly by fate. "His plants are the most important thing in his life," she added to further excuse Devin's behavior.

Colin regarded her dryly. "I'd have thought you'd be the most important thing in his life." It suddenly occurred to him that perhaps Madaline hadn't proved to be the perfect wife. The thought brought a sense of satisfaction. *I'm probably lucky I didn't end up with her,* he mused. Turning away, he walked toward the other men before she had a chance to respond.

Madaline watched him go. She'd seen the cynical gleam in his eyes and heard the implication in his voice that perhaps she wasn't the best wife in the world. Well, she didn't care what he thought of her!

Her gaze shifted toward the cliff edge. *Sanctuary Ridge.* The name played through her mind. She remembered the day she'd christened this place. It was during her second date with Colin. Their first date had been on a Saturday night. She'd felt awkward at first. She wasn't used to feeling awkward on dates. It wasn't that she had many; it was just that none of the boys she knew particularly interested her. But Colin was different.

On that first date, as they sat down in the movie theater and his shoulder brushed hers, a surge of heat had swept through her. About halfway through the show, when his hand had closed over hers, her breath had locked in her lungs and a hot rush of excitement had spread through her. She'd barely noticed the rest of the movie. Of course, she hadn't wanted him to guess what a strong effect he was having on her, so she'd kept her eyes on the screen, but it was Colin that her attention was focused on. She was thrilled by the strength of his work-roughened hand. Unable to control the urge, she shifted in her seat, a little movement as if she was feeling slightly stiff, but it brought her shoulder into firmer contact with his. The hard muscles enticed her, and she found herself wondering what it would feel like to have him holding her.

By the time they left the movie, she was thoroughly shaken. Afterward, they'd gone to the local café for some ice cream. Somehow she'd managed to make small talk about the movie, his work, her school, even the weather. But it wasn't easy. She kept finding herself drawn into the dark depths of his brown eyes and she just wanted to sit and stare at him. She was a college girl, not some silly immature high-school freshman, she kept reminding herself. But that didn't curb the nervousness she experienced as Colin walked her home. As hard as she tried not to, she kept wondering if he was going to kiss her. Even more, she wanted him to.

And he had. But his manner wasn't passionate or even forceful. He didn't even put his arms around her. He simply leaned down and kissed her lightly on the lips. Still, the contact sent a surge of excitement through her that caused her toes to curl with delight.

"I had a nice time," he said. He was studying her as if her response was important.

"I did, too," she replied honestly, and been rewarded by a crooked smile that caused a warm hard knot to form in her abdomen.

"I'd like to take you out again," he said, his voice holding a question.

"The weather is supposed to be clear tomorrow. It would be a nice day for a picnic," she suggested, then flushed. She'd never been this forward before, but she wanted to see him again so badly it was almost a physical need.

The brown of his eyes seemed to deepen. "I could pick you up around two."

"Two would be fine," she agreed.

That night, he'd filled her dreams. The next morning in church, she hadn't been able to stop herself from glancing covertly toward him several times. When she caught him looking at her, she experienced a rush of delight. But it had died a quick death. His gaze had been guarded, causing her to wonder if he was sorry he'd made a second date with her. Maybe after he'd left her the night before, he'd realized what a boring time he'd had and was regretting having agreed to spend an afternoon with her. Well, she wouldn't put him through any agony. If he wanted out of the date, she'd be happy to let him out of it.

"Is something going on between you and Colin Darnell?" Devin had asked her after church. As usual he'd been sitting with his family in the pew behind the one Madaline and her family normally occupied. She wasn't surprised he'd noticed the exchange of glances between her and Colin. It had been her experience that Devin noticed nearly everything that went on around him.

Once more she found herself irritated by the "big brother" role he'd assumed in her life. But she'd allowed him to play it for so long it didn't seem fair to hold it against him. "I don't think so," she replied.

Devin's expression became protective. "He didn't try anything unpleasant on your date last night, did he?" he demanded.

"He was a perfect gentleman," she assured him. She felt a prickling on the side of her neck and glanced past Devin's shoulder to find Colin watching her. This time the cold indifference on his face convinced her he was having second thoughts about their date that afternoon.

"Are you going to be seeing him again?" Devin persisted.

Madaline met his gaze levelly. "No, I don't think so."

All during Sunday dinner with her parents, Madaline told herself she was better off staying away from Colin Darnell. The stirrings he caused in her were too strong to be real or lasting. They had to be some sort of body-chemistry imbalance.

Nevertheless, she packed a picnic basket. The feelings she was experiencing made her restless and on edge. Once she'd freed Colin from their date, she intended to find a quiet place, have a solitary picnic and get her emotions back in order.

When Colin arrived, she was waiting on her porch. Leaving the picnic basket on the porch swing, she walked out to his pickup truck to meet him.

"You forgot our picnic," he said as she reached him. He'd climbed out of the cab and was regarding her cynically. "Have you decided you'd rather spend the afternoon with someone else? Devin maybe?"

She remembered seeing Colin's watching her with Devin after church. For a brief moment she found herself wanting to believe he was jealous, but then she reminded herself of the guarded expression she'd seen on his face during the service. It was only his pride talking, she decided. Her shoulders stiffened and she faced him squarely. "No, I haven't made any other plans. But I figured you were having second thoughts about our date. You didn't seem all that pleased to see me this morning."

His jaw tensed. "Truth is, I have been having second thoughts and third thoughts and even a few fourth thoughts."

Madaline's stomach knotted. *You knew he wanted out of the date,* she berated herself. *At least he's being honest.* She shoved her hands into the pockets of her denim shorts and forced indifference into her voice. "Then consider your afternoon your own. I've never forced my company on anyone who didn't want it, and I don't intend to start now." But as she turned to walk away, his hand closed around her arm.

"That didn't come out the way I intended." A self-consciousness came over his features. "I do want to spend the afternoon with you. I guess what's bothering me is how *much* I want to. It sort of scares me."

Her heart pounded wildly as she once again found herself drawn into the warm depths of his eyes. "I know what you mean," she said, then realizing the admission she'd just made, she flushed and jerked her gaze away. "I'd better go get the picnic basket."

"Yeah," he replied, releasing her abruptly and looking embarrassed, as if maybe he'd said too much.

A silence fell between them as she returned with the basket and climbed into the cab of the pickup. She wanted to say something, but the words kept getting stuck in her throat. *Well, this ought to cure him of wanting to date me,* she chided herself.

As they drove out of town, he suddenly broke the silence between them. "I was wondering if you'd mind if I called you Maggie." He glanced at her momentarily, an uneasy expression on his face, then quickly returned his attention to the road. "Madaline sounds so formal. Doesn't sound like the name of a female who'd give me two seconds of her time."

She'd never liked to be called Maggie before, but when Colin said it, it felt right. "Sure," she replied.

They parked by the stile bridging Zebulon's fence and climbed to the clearing on the ridge above the lake.

"I've never brought anyone else up here," he said as they sat resting and cooling off after the uphill hike. "It's always been my own private place."

"Your sanctuary," she said, pleased that she was the first person he'd wanted to bring here.

"Yeah, guess you could call it that," he replied. Then he asked her about her studies. When she told him that she was going to be an architect, they designed a house, scraping out floor plans in the rocky soil.

Whenever his hands or arms had brushed against her, she'd felt as if an electrical charge had raced through her. Even though she was continually unnerved by the strength of her reactions to him, she would not have wanted to be anywhere else. It had felt so natural being there with him, as if this was where she'd always belonged. Later that evening, as they'd sat eating their picnic dinner, it had occurred to her that being here with Colin was like being in a world apart from everyone else. But she hadn't felt isolated. Instead, she'd felt cozy and safe. "I christen this place Sanctuary Ridge," she'd said, pouring a little of her lemonade on the ground....

Madaline scowled at this memory. The name had been an appropriate one, but it had meant something entirely different to her than it had to Colin.

"And the sooner this house is built and I can put Colin Darnell out of my life, the better," she muttered, turning her full attention to the survey team.

Chapter Five

Driving home for lunch, Madaline recalled how Devin had tried to warn her about Colin from the start.

When she'd left for work the day after that long-ago picnic with Colin, Devin had been waiting outside to walk with her. "I came by yesterday afternoon to see if you wanted to go for a drive," he'd said, regarding her worriedly. "Your mother told me you had a date with Colin Darnell. I thought you said you weren't going to see him again."

She remembered feeling stifled by his overprotective attitude that hot summer morning. "I changed my mind," she'd replied sharply.

"I'm sorry," Devin apologized quickly, looking dismayed to have angered her. "I didn't mean to pry. But I've thought of you as my kid sister for too long. It's become a natural habit with me." He smiled so charmingly that she immediately regretted snapping at him.

"You can be a bit smothering at times," she cautioned, but her anger was gone, and she smiled to let him know that she forgave him.

His expression became serious again. "I don't mean to make you feel smothered, but I just don't want to see you get hurt." He regarded her closely. "I've never pictured you and Colin Darnell together."

She smiled sheepishly and her voice took on a confidential air. "I have to admit that I've sort of felt an attraction to him through the years, but I never thought he'd ever give me a second glance."

"Just promise me you'll go slowly," Devin had pleaded. "I've always thought Colin was a bit strange."

Madaline glared at him. "There is nothing strange about Colin." She continued to scowl at him as another truth dawned on her. "You've never liked anyone I've dated."

"That's not true." A sudden mischievousness entered Devin's eyes. "I liked Claude Mays."

"I never dated Claude Mays. He's so shy he still can't talk to a girl without stammering," she returned tartly.

"Oh." Devin screwed his face into a look of perplexity. Then he grinned. "I guess I've just always thought he would be the perfect date for you. He'd be too afraid to even hold your hand."

Madaline felt laughter building. She'd never been able to stay mad at Devin. "Please stop worrying about me," she requested in gentler tones. "Really, I'm perfectly capable of making sane decisions."

"Well, I should hope so," he replied, taking on the manner of a father speaking to his child. "I've certainly tried to raise you right."

Madaline had laughed outright then, and that had been the end of their discussion of Colin for that day.

"I would have been smart to have heeded his advice," she said ruefully now as she turned into the drive that led to Devin's home. This place had proved to be her real sanctuary. *Or maybe it's more of a hiding place,* she corrected.

Devin came out to greet her as she parked and got out of the car. "How did this morning go?" he asked. "I heard Colin was back in town."

"He is, but the morning went just fine, anyway," she assured him, deciding not to add that her nerves were totally frayed. She'd been so certain she could make herself feel only indifference toward Colin, but she'd experienced that old attraction as strongly as ever while watching him work with the surveyors.

Devin didn't look convinced. "Colin isn't trying to rekindle the old flame between you two, is he?" Quickly he added, "I want you to find a real husband one day, but I want him to be someone respectable and trustworthy."

Madaline forced a smile. "I can promise you that Colin is not the least bit interested in resurrecting the past, and neither am I."

Devin smiled and gave her hand a squeeze. "I want the best for you, Madaline. I want your life to be a happy one."

Colin stood looking at the view from the ridge. He was beginning to question his sanity. Building a house was a big undertaking, one that involved a great deal of time and money. Surely he could have come up with a simpler ploy to check on Maggie. He tried to rationalize by telling himself that since the first time he'd stood on this ridge, he'd wanted to build a home here. But the truth was that deciding to build this house had been an impulse, one so strong he'd had to act on it. It had been as if something deep down inside was pulling him back to Smytheshire, back to this ridge.

"Just like when I asked Maggie out on that first date," he muttered. That impulse had proved to be a disaster. "And this one may, too," he added grimly.

His jaw tensed so hard it almost locked. Just *seeing* her again was difficult enough; *working* with her was going to be impossible. He knew he should feel nothing but contempt for her. He'd been a game to her. Still, just a glimpse of her could ignite the flames of desire in him.

He pulled the letter out of his pocket and reread it. How the devil did he think he was going to help her anyway? Maybe it was time to do what he should have done in the first place. Maybe it was time to talk to Maggie. He shook his head at his duplicity. She was Madaline Smythe, not the "Maggie" he thought he'd known. She never really *was* "Maggie," he told himself sternly.

But no matter how hard he tried, he couldn't stop remembering the woman he'd once thought she was. It was that image that had brought him back to town. Calling himself two times a fool, he shoved the letter back into his pocket and started down the side of the mountain.

Madaline entered her office and breathed a sigh of relief. Samantha had called while she was home having lunch. Her secretary wasn't feeling well and wanted to let Madaline know she was taking the rest of the day off. And with Colin to oversee the surveyors, Madaline decided that they didn't need her. This meant she had the whole afternoon to herself. She hated to admit that being around Colin unnerved her so badly that she was desperate for some time alone, but it was the truth.

Seating herself at her desk, Madaline glanced through her phone messages. There was nothing that needed her immediate attention. She turned to her mail. On top of the stack of what was obviously mostly advertisements, was a letter with the word "personal" printed in bright red ink on the front. Her name and address were also printed in a neat precise hand. There was no return address, but it was postmarked from a nearby town.

Curious, she opened it. Inside, on a sheet of paper, printed in the same precise hand was:

> Virginity can be hazardous to your health. Live life to the fullest. Have an affair.

Her stomach began to churn. "This has got to be some sort of sick practical joke," she muttered. "Every woman in town probably got this same message." She crumpled the paper in her hand and started to throw it away. But she stopped before the action was completed. She uncrumpled the note and smoothed it out as best she could. Then she studied it for any clue as to who the writer might be. There was none.

The bell that signaled someone had entered the outer office rang. Her whole body tensed. She scowled at herself. It was stupid to let these silly warnings bother her.

She was just rising to go see who had entered when Colin stalked through her door. The grim expression on his face fit her mood. Immediately the atmosphere became charged as if for battle. His presence was the real problem, she thought. It had her overreacting to everything.

"We need to have a little talk," he growled, striding across the room and coming to an abrupt halt in front of her desk.

"Is there a problem with the design of the house?" she asked curtly. Then she heard herself adding, "Maybe you should find a new architect." From the minute he'd stepped through her door a week ago, she'd been wanting to suggest this, but pride had kept her silent. She didn't want him to guess how much he disturbed her. But now that it was said, she stood barely breathing, hoping he would agree.

"Maybe I should," he conceded. He felt like a fool. The cool anger on her face was enough to convince him that she neither needed nor wanted him in her life. Abruptly he made a decision. He'd tell her about the letter he'd received, then he'd get out of Smytheshire, return to Boston and never look back. Admittedly he'd already signed contracts to have the house built. If he couldn't get out of them, he knew the Kolby brothers would do a good job on their own. When the house was finished, his parents could use it, and when Zebulon died, he'd sell it. But he'd never live in it.

As he reached for the note in his pocket, his gaze flickered to her desktop and he stopped in midmotion. The printing on the envelope there looked very familiar. His attention shifted to the piece of paper that had obviously been crumpled, then flattened.

Madaline followed his line of vision. Quickly she leaned forward, putting a hand over the message on the paper. "Can I consider myself fired?" she asked.

Her movement had brought her face closer to his. For one brief instant he'd seen the panic in her eyes. Now she was glaring at him. Clearly this time it wasn't him that had frightened her. His gaze shifted back to her hand. "Some unpleasant news?" he asked, nodding toward the paper she was attempting to hide.

"No." Mentally she cursed herself. The word had come out too sharply. Those brown eyes of his were narrowed on her now. "It's just someone's idea of a practical joke," she said, attempting to force indifference into her voice.

It was plain to see she was rattled, Colin observed. It was equally plain she didn't want to discuss this with him. But he'd been pulled into this game or joke or whatever it was, and he wanted to know what the punch line was. "You're not laughing," he said.

"I don't find it funny."

Colin considered ripping the paper out from under her hand. That, however, he decided, could be dangerous. She reminded him of a she-cat prepared for battle. Maggie had never been the docile sort, he mused.

"I'll trade you my letter for yours," he offered, reaching into his pocket and pulling out the folded envelope written in the same hand as the one on her desk.

Madaline's eyes rounded in shock. "*Your* letter?"

She looked so shaken he wished he'd approached this with a bit more diplomacy. But it was too late for that. "Trade?" He extended his letter toward her with one hand while reaching for hers with the other.

Madaline stood frozen. What could Colin Darnell possibly have to do with anything that involved her virginity? Use caution, she ordered herself. "I'll read your letter and then I'll decide if you need to read mine," she said, reaching for his envelope while still keeping one hand firmly over the paper on her desk.

"No deal." Colin raised his arm, putting his envelope out of her reach. "It has to be an even trade."

She glared at him. "You always did have a stubborn streak in you."

"I'm surprised you recall anything at all about me," he returned. "You cut me out of your life so easily and so quickly I figured you'd barely remember I existed." Damn, he cursed himself. Why did he keep bringing up the past? She might get the foolish notion he still cared for her. And he didn't, he added with stern conviction.

Madaline experienced a rush of regret. She should have faced him all those years ago with what she knew. But what difference would it have made? her rational side argued. "I didn't see any sense in continuing with a relationship that couldn't last."

You knew from the beginning you were a fool to think you could compete with what Devin could give her, he ridiculed himself. The past was dead and gone. Right now, all that was important was finding out what kind of game was being played, who was playing it, and why he had been brought in as one of the players. "Your letter for mine," he stated again.

It occurred to Madaline that his letter might not have anything to do with her. Maybe whoever was sending these was simply sending random accusations to see if anyone would react. She recalled that ploy being used in an Agatha Christie novel once. "I'm really not interested in exchanging letters," she said.

That she appeared so desperate to hide whatever was in her letter made Colin more determined than ever to pursue this. "You're mentioned in my letter," he said in a tone that suggested she should be interested.

Madaline's stomach began to churn. "Please, let me see it," she requested tightly.

For a moment she went so white Colin thought she might faint. He could see that whatever was going on had her really upset. Relenting, he handed her his envelope.

Quickly she turned the crumpled sheet on her desk over so that the writing wasn't exposed. Then, taking his letter, she opened it and read the contents. Relief spread through her. It was nonspecific; just saying that she needed help from a friend. Glad she hadn't let him read her letter, she put his letter back into its envelope. But before returning the envelope to him, she glanced at the postmark. It was from Griswoldville, the same town her letter had come from. Then she noticed the date. "You got this weeks ago." Her brow wrinkled. "About the time you decided to build the house here."

Pride refused to allow him to let her guess that he had been honestly concerned about her. "I figured I'd be the last person you'd look to for help, but the letter got me thinking about my old hometown. My parents have been complaining about missing the change of seasons down in Florida. And I've always wanted to build a house on that ridge. The more I thought about it, the more it seemed that now was as good a time as any to build a place here. My parents could use it when they wanted a change of climate, and I'd have it as a retreat." He shrugged as if what he said next was of little consequence to him. "I just figured I'd sort of look into this as long as I was here. It did arouse my curiosity." *And remember what curiosity did to the cat,* he ridiculed himself. Aloud he added dryly, "I couldn't stop wondering what kind of help Devin Smythe's wife could possibly need from me."

His curiosity might have brought him here, but his manner and tone made it clear he would rather be walking over hot coals, Madaline thought. And he was right. He was the last person she would feel safe turning to for help. "None," she replied. "It's all just a silly prank."

Colin told himself to leave. He'd shown her the warning he'd received, and she was telling him to get out. And, he reminded himself, she had Devin to look after her. But he still wanted to know what kind of a prank could have her so thoroughly shaken. He knew it wasn't gentlemanly, but instead of accepting the envelope she was handing him, he abruptly changed direction and snatched up the crumpled sheet of paper.

"No!" The word came out in a panicked gasp as Madaline made a grab for the letter. She missed.

"Fair's fair," Colin said, stepping back well out of her reach. "I let you read mine." His jaw tensed. "Now it's my turn to see what kind of a joke has you so upset."

Calm down, Madaline ordered herself. *Think!*

Colin read the message. Then he read it again. Scowling, he turned his attention back to her. "This doesn't make any sense. You're a married woman."

Madaline schooled her features into an expression of righteous indignation. "I told you it was a sick practical joke."

Colin studied her. He was certain the panic he'd seen on her face had been real. "I don't understand why something like this would upset you so badly," he said, voicing his thoughts aloud.

"I simply don't like nasty pranks." *You're doing great,* she commended herself. *Just stay calm.* She reached for the crumpled paper. "I'd appreciate if you'd return that to me. I'd also appreciate it if you wouldn't mention this to anyone. I don't like being the brunt of false gossip."

Colin saw her hand tremble. It was only a slight shakiness; still, it caused him to study her even more closely. A possible explanation suddenly dawned on him. It didn't seem probable, but it would explain her behavior. "A person could get the impression that there is some truth to the writer's claim that you haven't consummated your marriage."

Retrieving the letter, Madaline again crumpled it as if preparing to throw it away. "That's ridiculous."

Colin wasn't sure exactly what it was—maybe there was some defensiveness in her voice, or maybe it was the way she suddenly diverted her eyes—but he was convinced she was lying. He didn't like bullying anyone, but whatever was going on, he'd been brought into it, and he was determined to learn the truth. His gaze traveled over her. "It does seem preposterous that Devin would not have claimed his husbandly rights," he conceded.

His inspection caused a rush of heat to spread through Madaline. Deep inside the fires of passion threatened to ignite. She wanted to scream with frustration. Of all the men in the world, why did Colin Darnell have to be the one who caused these stirrings within her? *Confirm his statement,* she ordered herself. But no words came out. He was moving toward her and it was taking every ounce of her strength not to bolt.

Colin had walked around the desk while he spoke. Reaching her, he cupped her face in his hands. "I want you to tell me the truth, Maggie," he said grimly.

Madaline's breath locked in her lungs. His touch was like fire, branding the imprint of his hands on her skin. She jerked away, taking a step back to put distance between them. "Go away." It was supposed to come out as an order; instead it sounded more like a plea.

Colin stood rigid. He'd never meant to touch her. His instincts had warned him it would be dangerous, and they were right. The soft feel of her had seriously threatened his control. He'd wanted to kiss her. Silently he laughed at himself. He'd wanted to do much more than that.

"Maybe I should leave," he conceded. He started toward the door. "I'll find my answers some other way."

Fresh panic swept through her. "No!"

Coming to a halt, he turned back toward her. "I will find out what's going on," he assured her. The look on her face reminded him of an animal caught in a trap. He hated himself for making her feel that way. A part of him warned that for his own sake, he should just walk away. But a stronger part refused to go. "I promise you that whatever you tell me will be held in the strictest confidence."

Deep down inside Madaline believed him, but he had fooled her once before.

Colin scowled at the indecision he read on her face. "I would never do anything to bring you harm," he swore gruffly. "But I want to know what's going on and I intend to find out."

Madaline saw the determined line of his jaw. If he started asking questions around town, there was sure to be gossip and speculation. Devin had been her protector for years; now it was her turn to protect him. "If you don't want to cause me any grief, then you'll forget this matter and not mention it to anyone."

As improbable as it seemed, Colin was now sure he was right. Taking a step toward her, he cupped her face in his hands again and forced her to look up at him. "You're still a virgin, aren't you."

The word no formed in her mind. But Colin was looking at her as if he could see into her very soul, and when she tried to spit out the denial, it stuck like a lump in her throat. She moved away from him and, rounding the desk, put it between them. She tried to think. Damn him, she cursed silently. But it was herself that truly angered her. She was completely rattled by him. Anyone else she could have faced down without a flicker of an eye.

Colin studied her grimly as an explanation entered his mind. "So Devin prefers the company of males to that of females," he said. "And you married him so he could put up the front of being straight."

Madaline glared at him. "That's absurd."

Colin couldn't doubt the indignation he saw on her face. He'd guessed wrong. That left only one other explanation why any red-blooded male who had the right would not have claimed Maggie. "Is he impotent?"

Madaline wanted to lie, but she was sure he would see through the deception. "You have no right to invade Devin's and my privacy this way," she seethed, attempting to avoid a direct answer.

But Colin wasn't fooled. He'd seen the flash of panic in her eyes. A bitter smile curled his lips. Clearly here was a woman who would do anything for money, even live like a nun.

"Did you know before you married him or learn about it afterward?" he asked.

Madaline felt cornered. She saw no recourse but to be honest with him and hope he had the decency to keep her and Devin's secret. "Before," she replied stiffly.

The bitter smile deepened. "I recall you telling me that you wanted children. I actually believed you. Does Devin know what a proficient liar he's married?"

Madaline glared at him. "*I* never lied to *you.*"

Colin scowled at the implication in her voice. "And I never lied to you."

She had to concede this could be the truth. He'd simply omitted a few things when he'd told her about himself. "This arrangement I have with Devin is not permanent," she said coolly. "I do plan to have a family one day."

I was lucky she set me free, Colin told himself. *The woman has no heart.* "Does Devin know this?"

"Of course." She read the disdain on his face. It was obvious he thought she was a conniving gold digger. Self-righteous indignation flashed in her eyes. "Devin needed a wife for a while, and he turned to me because we're friends. Brian Smythe is not a man who accepts imperfections in members of his own family, especially his grandson. It's likely he would disown Devin if he knew the truth."

"And so you married Devin to make it look as if he was virile." A cynical note entered his voice. "It would seem that Devin isn't above a little deceit."

His condemning attitude rankled. "Devin's impotency is not his fault. Because of it, he's been robbed of the chance to father children of his own. This has been a hard blow to him, but he's learned to live with it. However, it isn't fair that his impotency should rob him of his inheritance, as well. At the moment, Devin lives on a very generous allowance provided by his father and grandfather.

His grandfather, however, does not like the idea of people waiting around for him to die so that they can have their own wealth. When Devin's father turned thirty, Brian settled a half of his estate on him. Since then, Brian Smythe has rebuilt his wealth to equal what it had been. He made it clear several years ago that he intended to give half of it to Devin when Devin reached his thirtieth birthday. But a little over three years ago, he added a further stipulation. He wanted Devin to marry."

Colin had to admit that, under the circumstances, he could not blame Devin for entering into this charade. But it was Maggie's reasons for agreeing to participate that taunted him. "And so Devin came to you." A cynical gleam entered Colin's eyes. "And you agreed to marry him out of the *goodness* of your heart."

Madaline faced him with cool dignity. He, of all people, had no right to pass judgment on her. She knew about his dark side. "No, I married him for his money," she said bluntly.

Colin blinked. He'd been sure that was the reason, but he'd never expected her to admit to it.

Madaline refused to add that she'd wanted the money for her mother, Molly, to ensure that she received the very best medical care. She had her pride. She would not justify herself to Colin Darnell.

"At least you're honest," he said, breaking the sudden silence that had fallen between them.

She continued to regard him coldly. "And now it's up to you to prove you have some decency by keeping your word." Refusing to allow him to guess how worried she was now that he knew the truth, a threat entered her voice. "If you do decide to reveal what I've told you, I'll swear it's a lie and so will Devin. It will be your word against ours, and Brian Smythe will believe *us*."

She was a formidable foe, Colin thought, his gaze traveling from the ice in her eyes down her rigid form. He felt an unexpected surge of jealousy that Devin commanded her loyalty. Then he reminded himself that it was not Devin but Devin's money that owned her allegiance, and the jealousy turned to scorn.

"You don't have to worry—I'll keep your secret," he said with a coolness that matched hers. A cynical gleam entered his eyes. "There *are* ways of correcting some forms of impotency."

The thought of sharing a bed with Devin left Madaline cold. If he had shown any signs of wanting an intimate relationship, she would never have agreed to the marriage. She regarded Colin haughtily. "Devin has always thought of me as a sister, not as a lover."

"And how have you always thought of him?" Colin heard himself demanding, then berated himself for asking. How she felt about any man should be of no interest to him.

"He's been like a brother to me," she replied honestly, then added firmly, "He's my best friend." The thought that at one time she'd envisioned Colin as her best friend, as well as her husband and lover, caused a sharp twist of pain. Angrily she ignored it.

Colin found himself wondering if she'd discussed him and his infatuation with her with Devin. They probably got a laugh out of it, he decided. "If I were in your place, I'd tell Devin about the letters. He should be warned, in case someone is trying to discredit him," he advised curtly, striding toward the door.

Before Madaline could respond, he was on his way through the outer office and out the front door. She drew a shaky breath as the door closed behind him. He was right. She had to tell Devin.

Going into the outer office, she went to the front window and watched Colin walk down the street. "For Devin's sake," she said tersely, "I hope at least some of the Colin Darnell I thought I knew was real."

Chapter Six

"Really, it's all right," Devin said soothingly. "Colin Darnell is not a threat. We can always claim that anything he says is simply jealousy and a desire for vengeance. After all, you did jilt him."

"I just hate the thought of your having any trouble, especially when you'll turn thirty in barely a month," she replied. *And I'll be able to leave,* she added to herself.

She and Devin were in his library. It was a totally enclosed room, with no windows. Built-in cherrywood bookshelves occupied nearly every inch of wall space. They were filled with volumes on horticulture, religion, medicine, astronomy and a smattering of other subjects. Many were very old, so old she was afraid even to touch them for fear they would fall apart in her hands. A circular furniture grouping with a sofa and four stuffed chairs, all upholstered in soft dark leather, was situated toward one end of the room. Devin's desk was at the other. A square area rug of oriental design lay beneath the furniture grouping.

The rest of the dark-stained plank floor was bare. In the center of the room was Devin's most prized possession—his herbarium file. It contained dried samples of plants from every species found in his garden and on his land, plus many others he'd collected in his travels. It was a very scholarly looking room, Madaline thought. It even smelled scholarly. And it was Devin's favorite place in the entire house. Madaline, however, always felt a bit claustrophobic when she was in here, and tonight the feeling was stronger than usual. Nervously she paced around the room.

"Do you know of anyone who would want to cause you trouble?" she asked.

"My grandfather has a brother. He's dead now, but I think there was a son. I honestly can't be certain. Grandfather and his brother had a falling-out years ago, when my father was still a child, and never spoke again. But I suppose there could be cousins around, and one of them might think that if I'm discredited he could worm his way into my grandfather's good graces." He frowned thoughtfully. "But I find it hard to believe anyone could have discovered my secret. Of course, there are the doctor's files. I suppose someone could have gotten a look at them—maybe bribed a nurse or sneaked into the office undetected. If that's the case then it would seem most likely that person is some distant relative looking to inherit. I don't think I've made any enemies who would hate me so much they'd use a ploy like this to get even, and I can't think of anyone who would play a practical joke of this magnitude."

His manner abruptly became one of concern for her. "I doubt if you are in any danger, but I don't want to take any chances. Your safety is the most important thing." He frowned. "I'd insist on calling Chief Brant immediately, but I'm pretty sure there's nothing he can do. No real threat has been made and with only one full-time deputy at his disposal, he couldn't put a guard on you even if he wanted to."

He hadn't said it, but Madaline knew he didn't relish the idea of explaining to the police chief why these notes and phone calls were so upsetting. Chief Brant had also grown up in Smytheshire and was only a few years older than Devin. Madaline was sure he was a man whose word could be respected and that he would never divulge Devin's secret, but it still would be humiliating for Devin.

Devin regarded her worriedly. "Maybe I should hire a private detective to guard you."

Madaline stopped her pacing and turned to face him. "Don't be ridiculous. You just said no threat has been made against me. And there's no reason in the world why my virginity should put me in any danger. These letters are absurd. I'm sure whoever is sending them simply wants us to react. If we don't, maybe he'll give up and go away."

"I admit that they do seem absurd. And not involving anyone else would be less embarrassing to me," Devin confessed, adding with apology in his voice, "also less risky." He frowned again. "But if the letters continue, I am going to get you some protection." His frown deepened. "And I don't understand why Colin Darnell has been brought into this."

Madaline was beginning to feel giddy from the strain of the day. "Maybe the author of the letters chose Colin to be the one I was to have the affair with." The thought was out before she'd even realized it had formed in her mind. Her own startled reaction to what she'd said was reflected in the shocked expression on Devin's face. Her laugh was brittle. "If that's the case, the writer is going to be sorely disappointed. Colin Darnell intensely dislikes me and I have no interest in him."

Devin looked relieved. "For your sake, I'm glad to hear that. I don't want to see you hurt by that man again."

"That is one thing you absolutely don't have to worry about," she assured him. The walls were beginning to feel as if they were closing in on her. She had to get out of there before she said something else ridiculous. "And now I'm tired. I think I'll go up to bed." Quickly she gave Devin a light kiss on the cheek, then left.

But she didn't go directly to her room. She was too tense to sleep. Turning down the corridor of the east wing, Madaline followed it until she reached the conservatory. This was her favorite place in the house. Whenever she came here, she felt as if she'd stepped into a huge beautifully decorated glass bubble. It was two stories high, to provide room for the trees that grew inside. These trees shaded the iron-and-wood benches spaced along the stone path that wound through the long glass structure. Flowering plants of many varieties were arranged throughout. In this room the air was warm and smelled sweet from the perfume of the blossoms. It was like being in a place of perpetual summer.

Darkness had fallen, but she didn't turn on the small lights that lined the stone path. The full moon, shining through the glass, provided her with all the illumination she needed to see her way. Seating herself on a bench in the midst of a cluster of blooming irises, she stared up at the star-filled sky beyond the glass enclosure. Her hands balled into fists in her lap. She was furious with herself. The thought of an affair with Colin Darnell was crazy. In the first place, she had no intention of having an affair with any man. When she was finally free of her obligation to Devin, she intended to find a husband and have a family. And in the second place, as she'd told Devin, Colin Darnell did not want to be a part of her life, and even if he did she didn't want him in it. Yet she couldn't get him out of her mind. After all this time, she could still remember the thrill of being held in his strong embrace.

As if suddenly aware of another presence, her gaze shifted downward from the stars and out toward the darkened landscape. Standing on the lawn, beyond her glass encasement, was a man. A huge old oak sheltered him from the moonlight, causing him to be more of a shadow than a discernible image. Then he stepped forward, and she saw that it was Colin.

After leaving Madaline's office that afternoon, Colin went back to Zebulon's place. He was staying with the old man while the work on his house was being done. To his relief, Zebulon was out. He wasn't in the mood to talk to anyone. He'd leave Zebulon a note. All he wanted was to pack and get out of town as quickly as possible. He'd shown Maggie the letter and had the answers he'd come to get. But instead of feeling as if he'd finally closed this chapter of his life, he was restless.

He'd been right about her all these years, he thought as he pulled out his suitcase and began to throw his things inside. She was coldhearted to the core.

The image of Maggie looking him in the eye, telling him that she'd married Devin for money, filled his mind. He stopped packing and paced over to the window. In spite of all the evidence, in spite of her own words, he wanted to believe that at least a part of the Maggie he'd known was real. "You're a fool, Colin Darnell," he muttered.

Instead of finishing his packing, he went out for a drive. He ended up at the café. Nothing about the place had changed since he and Maggie used to go there. The tables were still covered with red-and-white-checked cloths. Even the vases of plastic flowers resembled ones that had sat on the tables four years ago. He ordered dinner but didn't eat much. He kept seeing Maggie sitting across from him, his

Maggie, with her open innocent smile and those green eyes that enticed him with their warm emerald glimmer.

Leaving the café, he knew what he had to do. He'd been avoiding going to Devin's. Now he knew he *had* to go there. He had to see Maggie in Devin's house. It was as if he needed this final evidence to free himself from her.

His restlessness stronger than ever, Colin chose to walk. He knew Devin's place was two miles out of town, but he didn't care. Tonight he needed the cool air and the exercise to help clear his mind. Colin was aware that all the land Smytheshire was built on had once belonged to the Smythes and that they still owned a great deal of the surrounding acreage. No one in town was sure how the Smythe ancestors had made their money. It was common knowledge, however, that they had some wealth when they came to America. Colin's father had speculated that they'd increased their holdings through investments in banking, mining, shipping and whatever else was a booming industry at the time. Now the Smythes pursued hobbies instead of jobs and let their money work for them.

Colin smiled cynically. Some parents gave their children cars when their offspring graduated from high school. Devin's parents had given him a car when he got his license at sixteen and a half. When he graduated from high school, he'd asked for his own home and they'd given him a mansion, along with several acres of land.

Colin paused as he reached the private drive leading to the house. He'd never actually seen Devin's place. It was set nearly half a mile from the main road, hidden by heavily wooded land. He'd heard how grand it was, mostly from the people who worked there. Devin didn't invite many guests to his home. Maggie had been one of the few regular visitors.

Colin's jaw tensed as he remembered the time he'd allowed his jealousy of her friendship with Devin to show.

He and Maggie had been dating for a month. In his mind, she'd become his girl. But on a Thursday afternoon in August, when he'd been putting new shingles on the roof of the post office, he'd seen her with Devin. They'd been laughing and talking as they walked down the street. Then they'd gone into the café. She had turned and waved to Colin. He'd waved back, then returned his attention to the shingles as if it didn't matter to him that she was with another man. But it *did* matter. It mattered a great deal.

That night, when he went to pick her up for their date, he decided that it was time to find out if she was taking their growing relationship as seriously as he was. "We need to talk," he said the moment they were alone in his truck.

She glanced toward him, an anxious expression on her face. "You sound serious."

He felt like a jealous idiot. "This isn't easy for me," he admitted gruffly.

There was a flash of hurt on her face, then a look of proud defiance came over her features. "If you're trying to tell me you're tired of my company, just say so." She reached for the handle of the door. "In fact, there's no reason for you to feel obligated to take me out tonight."

Reaching across her, he caught her hand before she could open the door. "That's not what I want. I'm not tired of your company. The truth is I'd like to spend all my time with you."

She smiled then, a shy, happy smile. "I like the sound of that."

He found it hard to think with her looking at him like that, but then Devin's image entered his mind. "I need to know where I stand with you, Maggie," he said stiffly. "I need to know if you still have feelings for Devin."

"I will always have feelings for Devin," she replied and Colin felt as if a knife had been driven into him and twisted. "Devin has been my friend for as long as I can remember," she continued. "But that's all he is—a friend."

The pain vanished in the warmth of her gaze. "I'm glad to hear that," he said, then heard himself confessing, "I've never been jealous before. But when I saw you with him today, I wanted to come down off that roof and tell him to go home and stay away from you."

An anxiousness entered her eyes. "I hope you're not going to ask me to stay away from him." A plea entered her voice. "He and I have been friends for too long. I can't turn away from him. He never complains, but I know he gets lonely."

Colin had never thought of himself as a possessive person, but at the moment he wanted to ask her to do just that—stay away from Devin. But he couldn't. He knew it wouldn't be fair. She had a right to have her own friends. And, he guessed it was true what she said about Devin's getting lonely. Colin hadn't gone away to college. His teachers had encouraged him, but his father's business had been going well and Colin was needed to help out. Colin had no regrets. He'd never liked studying. He enjoyed working with his hands and he made a decent living—enough to support a wife and family.

But why Devin hadn't gone to college had always puzzled him. Money hadn't been a problem and Devin was smart enough. But instead, Devin had hired tutors and continued his studies privately. He wasn't a recluse exactly, but his circle of friends was small. In fact, Maggie was the only one Colin could think of who Devin spent any real amount of time with.

"No, I won't ask you to stop seeing him," he said. "But don't get angry with me if I act a little jealous once in a while," he cautioned.

"I sort of like the idea of your being a little jealous," she replied with a coquettish grin.

He'd kissed her then. . . .

Colin trembled. Just the memory of that kiss caused a rush of heat to spread through him. "Damn!" he cursed. Vanquishing the image of the past from his mind, he strode up the private drive.

It's no wonder she didn't want to give up her friendship with Devin, he thought cynically as Devin's home came into view. The place was most definitely grand. Not only was the house itself a sprawling three-story brick affair, but it was surrounded by gardens and manicured lawns.

There wasn't any need for him to go any farther, he decided. He couldn't condemn Maggie for being tempted by this kind of opulence. Still, he felt an anger. He'd believed her when she'd claimed to be indifferent to Devin's wealth. *I guess when I started talking about marriage and she realized that if she accepted she'd be giving up the chance for all this, she decided that marrying me was too much of a sacrifice,* he thought acidly.

Then he saw her. The huge glass doom fitted against the house had caught his attention, and although he'd told himself to leave, instead, he'd wandered toward it. Only moonlight illuminated the interior. But even though she was only a shadowy figure, he knew it was Maggie. He watched her walk slowly through the plant filled room until she reached the center. Once there, she sat down and turned her attention skyward.

Like a bird in a gilded cage, he thought, then laughed at himself for this old cliché. Still, he found himself wondering if she was really happy. *Her happiness is of no concern to me,* he assured himself. He felt more than saw her attention shift toward him. When she got up abruptly, he knew she'd seen him.

Madaline stood staring out at the man on the lawn. It occurred to her that she should be frightened. But the fear refused to come. Instead, the desire to walk out into his arms was so strong it caused a tremor to run through her body. The glass walls she had always thought of as housing a fairyland of beauty suddenly seemed like a prison.

Against his will, Colin's legs carried him closer. Maggie had moved forward, and now the moonlight struck her fully. In the dimness, he still could not see her features, but he saw her hand reach out toward him. He felt an almost overwhelming urge to reach through the glass barrier and claim her for his own.

Tears of frustration burned in Madaline's eyes. Why couldn't Colin have been the kind of man she'd thought he was? Why did he have to have that dark side? Suddenly realizing she was reaching out toward him, she abruptly jerked back her hand.

Colin felt her rejection as sharply as if she'd slapped him. A shaft of cold shot through him.

"Madaline, are you all right?"

She swung around as the floor lights along the path were suddenly turned on. Devin was coming toward her with Mrs. Grayson trailing behind. The concern Madaline saw on Devin's face was matched on the housekeeper's motherly countenance. "Yes, I'm fine," she replied, wondering what was causing them to be so anxious.

"Mrs. Grayson says she saw a prowler," Devin explained as he reached her.

Suddenly the housekeeper let out a small scream and pointed toward the lawn. Her plump figure trembled and fear filled her eyes. "I did see someone," she choked out.

"It's Colin," Madaline said with schooled indifference. "I was just on my way to find out why he's here." This, she admitted to herself, was a lie. It was the reasonable thing to do, but she knew that if Devin hadn't arrived, she would never have left her glass shelter. It wasn't a fear of Colin that had her wanting to remain apart from

him; it was a fear of herself and the emotional turmoil brewing within her. She wanted to feel nothing but contempt for him. Instead she was drawn toward him as if by an invisible magnet so strong it took all of her strength to fight it.

"We'll both go see what he wants," Devin said, taking the lead toward the door that opened out onto the small flagstone patio facing the lawn. Glancing over his shoulder, he added, "Please wait here, Mrs. Grayson."

The woman nodded and Madaline had the impression the housekeeper was poised to run for help at any moment.

Colin watched them approaching. He felt like an intruder. I am an intruder, he pointed out to himself with cynical humor. And he'd been caught. Just play this out casually, he directed himself.

"Evening," he said, approaching the patio as Madaline and Devin stepped out.

"What can we do for you?" Devin asked.

Colin noted that Devin's tone was polite but cold. Obviously Devin didn't like his being here. "I was just out for a stroll and ended up on your property," Colin replied. This was loosely the truth, he reasoned. "I've never seen your place. Thought I'd just take a quick look. Thought I might get some ideas for future projects in Boston."

Devin regarded him doubtfully. "You can see it much better in the daylight."

"You've got a point," Colin conceded. He wanted to ask if Maggie had told Devin about the letters, but he refrained. For the moment, anyway, he'd leave that decision up to her.

"Would you like a quick tour of the inside?" Devin offered unexpectedly.

Madaline's stomach knotted. A superior edge had entered Devin's voice. He was patronizing Colin, almost mocking him, and this bothered her. She wanted to come to Colin's aid, and that surprised her. *Colin Darnell doesn't need or want my help,* she reminded herself curtly.

Colin had never thought of himself as a violent man, but at this moment he wanted to punch Devin Smythe in the mouth. Instead, he smiled an easy smile. "No, thanks." He glanced at his watch as if he had another appointment. "It's getting late." A challenge shone in his eyes. "Some other time, maybe."

Devin smiled back. "Anytime."

They reminded Madaline of two warriors squaring off for battle. They were both proud men, she knew, and each in his own way was feeling threatened. She guessed that Colin was not used to being caught trespassing. As for Devin, it had to be hard for him to face a man who knew his secret. Guilt assailed her. Devin's discomfort was her fault, and he'd always been so kind and good to her.

"Good night," Colin said, his gaze flickering over the two of them.

"Good night," Devin replied.

Madaline heard herself adding a third cool "Good night."

Then Colin turned and walked away.

"I'm really sorry about everything," Madaline said as she stood beside Devin and watched Colin disappearing down the drive. "I never should have told him," she apologized again.

Devin breathed a tired sigh, then gave her an encouraging smile. "It's not your fault." He suddenly frowned anxiously. "I suppose I should have been more cordial. Colin could make things a little difficult for us."

There was nothing but shadows in the distance now. Still, Maggie stared in the direction in which Colin had gone. "The fact that he didn't mention the letters or your secret is a sign that he's keeping his word about being discreet."

Suddenly realizing she felt angered that Devin had questioned Colin's integrity and that anger had made her tone impatient, she scowled at herself. Devin had every right to question Colin's trustworthiness. "I seem to be a little on edge," she quickly apologized. "I didn't mean to sound so sharp."

Devin had opened the door. Stepping aside, he motioned for her to enter. "I've noticed that you've been rather uneasy these days," he said, following her inside. His tone was solicitous. "If Colin's presence upsets you, perhaps you should insist that he hire another architect."

"I'd be wary of any man who went sneaking around my home in the middle of the night," Mrs. Grayson cautioned, glancing toward the lawn as if afraid Colin might reappear at any moment.

Madaline felt real anger this time. She'd totally forgotten about the housekeeper's presence. She didn't mind Devin's protectiveness. She'd grown used to it through the years. But she objected to anyone else's criticizing Colin, and she didn't like Devin's making it sound as if she was afraid of Colin, especially in front of a witness.

"Colin doesn't bother me," she replied coolly. "Besides, I have a contract."

Mrs. Grayson shook her head. "If you ask me, that man is trouble."

"I'm sure I can handle him," Madaline replied firmly.

Devin smiled and put his arm around her shoulders. "I'm sure you can."

Mrs. Grayson gave a small impatient snort. "It's always been my creed to stay away from trouble whenever possible."

"Mrs. Grayson," Devin asked, "Don't you have somewhere else you should be at this moment?"

"Yes, sir," she replied, adding primly, "In my bed, hopefully not having to worry about any more prowlers."

Madaline frowned impatiently. "I'm sure we're all safe here."

"Good night, Mrs. Grayson," Devin said with firm dismissal.

Mrs. Grayson looked properly chastised. "Good night, Mr. Devin, Mrs. Smythe," she responded stiffly, then turned and walked toward the door. "I was merely trying to give them the benefit of my years of experience," they heard her muttering. "These young people today all think they know everything...."

"I really am concerned about you," Devin said when he and Madaline were alone. "Contracts can be broken."

"I can handle working with Colin Darnell," Madaline assured him. She just wished she felt as confident as she sounded.

As Colin walked back toward town, he told himself again that he should pack and leave and never look back. But someone had appointed him Madaline Smythe's protector. He didn't want the job. He wasn't even certain she *needed* protecting. She most certainly was a woman who knew how to take care of herself. But until he had a few more answers, he knew he was going to stay.

Chapter Seven

Madaline awoke the next morning feeling more exhausted than when she had gone to bed. A groan of frustration escaped her as she raked her hair away from her face with her fingers and forced herself to sit up. All night Colin had haunted her dreams. In them, he'd kissed her and her body had flamed with passion. Even now, when she was fully awake, an aching desire to be in his arms tormented her.

She looked toward the window. Outside, it was still dark. She glanced at the clock on the bedside table. It would be sunrise soon.

Too restless to stay in bed, she rose and dressed in a pair of old jeans, a sweatshirt and sneakers. She wanted a cup of coffee, but she didn't want to take the chance of waking Mrs. Grayson or Claire. Neither would normally be up for another hour, and Madaline didn't want to disturb their rest. Besides, she needed to be alone. The walls of her room, the walls of this *house,* felt like a cage.

I can make myself some coffee at my office, she decided, grabbing her purse and heading toward the door.

But she didn't drive to her office. She continued through town, instead. She hadn't thought about where she was going until she found herself at the spot where the stile had provided access to Zebulon's property. Only now that property belonged to Colin, and the fence in this section had been torn down. The crew that had cleared the land for the house had also cleared a gently winding roadway leading up to the ridge. But the roadway was still an unpaved dirt track and had been deeply rutted by the trucks that had hauled the cut lumber away. It was not safe for a car to travel.

The first rays of sunlight were beginning to peek over the horizon as she parked at the side of the main road and hiked up to the ridge. Once there, she stood looking out over the landscape as the shadows faded in the dawn light. She didn't know why she had come. She felt as if she was looking for something but she wasn't certain what.

"The last time I came searching for something up here, I had a very unpleasant surprise," she reminded herself aloud.

"Is this a private conversation or can anyone join in?"

Madaline twisted around abruptly to discover Colin walking toward her. Every muscle in her body tensed with frustration. A part of her wanted to run into his arms, but another part knew she could never accept his dark side. Besides, he had nothing but contempt for her. He'd probably rather hold a rattlesnake than her, she thought. "Don't you have a business in Boston to run?" she heard herself asking sharply.

When Colin had first seen Maggie standing there he'd almost thought he was hallucinating. She was outlined by the morning sky and dressed in old clothes. Her hair, touched as it was by the sunlight, was hanging loose and flowing over her shoulders. All night, she'd filled his dreams. When he'd woken, a restlessness had brought him to this old meeting place of theirs. He'd come by a back path from Zebulon's place, so he hadn't seen her car. Finding her there was unexpected. It was also clear that she hadn't expected him nor was she pleased he had come. The meaning behind her words couldn't have been any clearer if she'd said, *Go back to Boston and leave me alone.* Which is exactly what he wanted to do, he assured himself. But first he needed a few more answers.

"I have a crew foreman I trust," he replied evenly, showing no offense at her blatant manner. "Thought I'd stick around until the foundation is laid, just in case there are any problems."

Madaline berated herself. She'd been rude. "It's your home. You're free to oversee the entire construction," she said levelly.

Colin's hands balled into fists. Up here, alone with her, the old memories were too strong to suppress. He had an overwhelming urge to demand how she could have acted so willing to spend the rest of her life with him, and then suddenly turned so completely against him that she'd refused even to speak to him. But he had his pride. Besides, he knew the answer. Down deep inside she had a heart of ice. *And if she gives me the right answers this morning, I won't even have to stay around to see the foundation laid,* he promised himself.

"Did you tell Devin about the letters?" he asked bluntly.

Recalling all that she had revealed to Colin the day before, Madaline felt a blush of embarrassment spreading up her neck. "Yes," she replied stiffly.

Colin saw the blush. Damn, he cursed under his breath, and a wave of protectiveness swept through him. How could she look so innocent and yet be so deceitful? "What action has he decided to take?" he demanded, hoping the answer would free him from any obligation to remain in Smytheshire.

"None, for the moment." The look of disapproval on Colin's face forced her to come to Devin's defense. "If we reacted it would only encourage the letter writer and could start rumors. Besides there've been no real threats made."

Colin scowled. "Considering how Devin has always hovered over you in the past, I expected to hear he'd hired a battalion of bodyguards for you." *At least, that's what I'd hoped for,* he added to himself. If that had been the case, there would have been no need for him to remain.

The cynical edge in Colin's voice irked Madaline. "If I thought I needed a bodyguard, Devin would provide one for me. I've always been able to count on him. He's been here for me whenever I needed a friend or a shoulder to lean on. Without him, I would have been alone—"

She stopped abruptly as a lump formed in her throat. Her back stiffened and she faced Colin with cold defiance. There was no reason she should have to justify herself or Devin to this man.

Suddenly remembering that she'd lost both her parents during the past four years, Colin felt like a heel. "I was sorry to hear about your mother and father," he said with honest sympathy.

She'd liked it better when he was being sarcastic, she decided. The unexpected softness in his eyes caused her stomach to knot, and she again found herself wanting to be in his arms.

"Madaline! You had me worried half out of my mind."

Madaline tensed as her gaze shifted toward the primitive roadway and she saw Devin coming toward them. He looked frantic, and a wave of guilt washed over her. "I'm sorry, I didn't mean to worry you."

But he wasn't looking at her. He was looking at Colin. "Colin." He said the name with curt greeting, acknowledging the other man's presence. Then he turned back to Madaline. "When I woke up and discovered you weren't in the house and your car was gone, I didn't know what to think. I tried calling your office. I was going to call Chief Brant, but on a hunch, I came here first." His gaze shifted between the two of them before coming back to rest on Madaline. "I've always trusted you to be honest with me. If you felt you needed to see Colin privately, you could have told me, instead of sneaking out. I might have tried to talk you out of it, but I wouldn't have forbidden it."

It was obvious to Colin that Devin thought this was some sort of lovers' clandestine meeting. It also occurred to Colin that if he'd been in Devin's shoes, he'd have been ready to do bodily harm to the man Maggie was meeting. But then, Devin and Maggie had a relationship based on monetary concerns, he reminded himself cynically.

Madaline glared at Devin. As usual, he was being understanding, but that didn't take the bite out of his words. "I didn't come up here to meet Colin," she said tightly. "I woke up and couldn't sleep. I was restless, so I went for a drive and ended up here. I didn't expect Colin to show up."

An expression of apology came over Devin's features. "I'm sorry. I was just so worried about you."

Devin's reasonable attitude was making Colin feel more and more awkward. "Zebulon will be expecting me for breakfast," he said. "So if you two will excuse me, I'll be on my way." He turned and strode out of the clearing.

Madaline watched his departure in silence. To her chagrin, a part of her wanted to go with him. Drawing a shaky breath, she forced her gaze away from him.

"I realize living like a nun must be difficult for you," Devin said, breaking the heavy stillness between them. "But it will only be for a little while longer."

Madaline turned to see him studying her. She didn't feel like smiling, but she forced an encouraging smile, anyway. "We have a deal and I promise you I will keep my end of it. I'll be your faithful wife until our marriage has officially ended."

Devin looked relieved. "I knew I could count on you. A scandal could ruin everything." Then his concern returned. "I love you like a sister, Madaline, and I want you to have everything you've ever dreamed of. But I had hoped you'd gotten over Colin Darnell."

Her jaw tensed. "I have."

Devin raised an eyebrow skeptically. "I saw the way you were looking at him as he walked away. I could have sworn you were wishing you could go with him."

"I was regretting that he wasn't the kind of man I thought he was when I fell in love with him," she replied, her gaze shifting once more to the path Colin had taken.

Devin nodded sympathetically. "I remember how your eyes glistened when you told me how much you cared for him. I also remember how devastated you were when you learned the truth about him."

Madaline swallowed hard. She hadn't been feeling well the night she'd discovered the truth, and what she'd learned had made her stomach churn. Just the memory caused a wave of nausea. "You don't have to concern yourself about Colin Darnell. He'll never be a part of my life."

Devin placed an arm around her shoulders. "I'm glad to hear that. He would only bring you sorrow." He gave her shoulders a brotherly squeeze. "Now come along. You look as if you could use some coffee and a bit of breakfast."

What I'd like is a good cry, she confessed to herself. *But that would be really stupid.* Her gaze traveled over the rocky surface on which she stood. A chill unrelated to the early-morning crispness in the air caused her to shiver.

"The coffee sounds like an excellent idea," she said, beginning to move toward the roadway.

For the next few days, she managed to avoid Colin. She told herself that this was for Devin's sake, that she didn't want to cause him any anxiety.

But that wasn't the complete truth, she finally admitted to herself one night at two in the morning when she couldn't sleep. Outside a storm was raging. Rain was pelting the house while the wind was bending trees until they seemed about to snap. Madaline stood in the darkness, looking out her window at the violent night.

She'd tried to sleep, but every time she closed her eyes Colin's image filled her mind. The Kolby brothers respected and liked Colin. So did the other men on the job. She'd seen it in their faces when they talked to him or about him with others. Cynically she wondered what they would think of him if they knew what she knew.

Hot tears burned at the back of her eyes. "Damn!" she cursed in a hushed voice. Having him in Smytheshire again hadn't worked out the way she'd hoped. She'd thought that seeing him again might help her put the past behind her, but instead, it haunted her more than ever. *Maybe the only way to finally be free is to face him, to tell him I know the truth about him,* she thought. This would mean revealing how much he'd hurt her. *But maybe a little catharsis is what I need.*

"Looks like the storm kept you awake last night," Devin observed sympathetically when Madaline, mauve circles under her eyes, joined him for breakfast the next morning.

She merely nodded as she took a sip of coffee. Through the years she had talked out a great many of her problems with Devin. Their discussions had helped her make important decisions. But what to do about Colin Darnell was a decision she'd have to make on her own.

Mrs. Grayson entered and smiled consolingly at Madaline. "You look a bit worse for the wear this morning."

Madaline grimaced into her coffee cup. Obviously she should have taken the time to put on some makeup, but she'd been too tired.

Mrs. Grayson's attention turned to Devin. "Charles came early to check the gardens. There's a bit of damage in the rose garden, and lightning split one of the oaks in the grove surrounding the herb garden."

Devin breathed a regretful sigh. "I suppose we shall lose the tree."

"I'm sorry," Madaline said, knowing how much he prized those ancient oaks.

Mrs. Grayson nodded in agreement. "It is a shame to lose one of those magnificent old trees." Then her voice took on a practical tone. "But we should consider ourselves lucky. We didn't suffer any real damage. When Charles arrived this morning, he told me that the big maple in old Mrs. Elberly's yard was split by the storm and half of it fell against her house. Tore a huge hole in the roof. He thinks it might have knocked out part of the living room wall, as well. Said it looked like a mess."

Madaline forgot about the oak as the image of the frail eighty-three-year-old woman came into her mind. "Was Mrs. Elberly hurt?"

"No." Mrs. Grayson smiled and shook her head. "Slept through the whole thing."

Madaline's eyes rounded in astonishment. "Slept through it?"

"Well, she's deaf as a politician the day after the election," Mrs. Grayson pointed out. "And lucky for her, her bedroom is at the other end of the house." She nodded her head to emphasize this good fortune. "Anyway, several of the neighbors woke up and went rushing over. Helen Ashbey has a key to the house in case of an emergency, and she and the others went in and got Mrs. Elberly out. Helen took her home with her."

"Have Claire pack a large basket of food," Madaline instructed. "I'll take it over there and see if I can be of any help."

Mrs. Grayson smiled brightly. "I knew you'd want to. The basket's already packed."

As Mrs. Grayson left, Devin rose from the table. "You go be the angel of mercy," he said, giving Madaline a light kiss on the cheek. "I'm going to see if I can salvage any of my tree and check the rest of the damage."

Watching him leave, Madaline frowned. It bothered her that he seemed more concerned about his plants than about Mrs. Elberly. But that was Devin's way, she reminded herself. He preferred to keep himself apart from people in general. And she couldn't fault him for that. Although on the surface he acted as if he had accepted his impotency and didn't let it bother him, she guessed that deep down inside it made him feel self-conscious. She also knew that if Mrs. Elberly required any financial aid, Devin would willingly give whatever was needed.

And, she reminded herself, his work with the plants wasn't totally for his own enjoyment. He had an extensive laboratory in which he was attempting to extract plant toxins with some hope that one day they would be useful to mankind.

Going up to her room, she changed into jeans and a sweatshirt. Recalling Devin's and Mrs. Grayson's remarks, she also took a moment to apply some makeup. "No sense in frightening people," she muttered, making an attempt to hide the circles under her eyes.

Turning onto Mrs. Elberly's street a little later, she saw several cars parked near the old woman's house. One of the things she liked best about this small community was the way people pulled together, she thought as she parked behind a station wagon. When someone needed help, people came to offer their services. But the smile on her face faded when she saw Colin's car.

"Why isn't he up on the ridge checking on his own property?" she grumbled. Granted, she'd decided she should face him, but she wasn't prepared to see him right now.

"Morning," Ray Kolby called out to her. He'd been heading toward his truck, but now he changed direction and walked toward her. "Hope you won't be upset," he said apologetically when he reached her. "I know you told us Colin's job was a rush, and we did go up there first thing this morning. But when we mentioned old Mrs. Elberly's house, Colin insisted we come here and work today. Luckily the damage isn't as bad as it looks. The roof's got a hole in it and there's water damage and some broken windows in the living room. But there wasn't any structural damage to the walls. We should have it completely repaired in a day or two."

Sending the Kolby brothers and their crew up here to help had been the right thing to do, Madaline conceded. It was what she would have expected of the Colin Darnell she'd fallen in love with. *The Colin Darnell I thought I knew,* she added.

"Was there any damage on the ridge?" she asked, hoping this small interruption to their work on Colin's house wouldn't slow the project by much.

"A couple of trees came down on top of the foundation we're laying," Ray replied. "It'll take a day to clear them. Then we can check more fully." He gave a shrug and added philosophically. "As Colin says, it's a good thing it happened before the house was built."

Madaline nodded. *Why should I have expected anything to go smoothly where Colin Darnell is concerned,* she mused. *It never has before.*

"Best be getting my tools and going up on that roof," Ray said. Before she could respond, he was already heading toward his truck.

A small wail sounded behind her. Turning, she saw Mrs. Elberly approaching. Arthritis caused the woman to move slowly, and she was leaning heavily on Helen Ashbey's arm. "My house," she was saying in a shaky voice. "Oh, my. Oh, my."

"Now don't you worry," Helen replied comfortingly. "All these people have come to repair it. In a couple of days it'll be as good as new." Seeing Madaline, she smiled brightly with relief. "Isn't that so?" Clearly she was looking for support to help ease the old woman's mind.

"Ray Kolby just told me that it's not nearly as bad as it looks," Madaline said reassuringly. "And Claire packed this basket to help feed the workers."

Mrs. Elberly managed a small smile. Suddenly a look of horror spread over her face. "Tom! Where's Tom! I've been so upset I completely forgot about him."

"Tom?" Madaline questioned, glancing at Helen.

"Her cat," Helen explained.

Mrs. Elberly had turned pale and she began moving toward her house. "Tom!" she called, her voice filled with panic. "Oh, how could I have forgotten about him?"

"You were badly shaken last night. The doctor insisted on giving you a sedative," Helen reminded her.

But Mrs. Elberly wasn't paying any attention. Instead, she scanned the yard and then the front porch. "Tom!" she called again.

"You looking for this guy?" Madaline saw Colin coming out of the house, a large calico cat in his arms. "Found him hunting around in the kitchen for his breakfast," he said.

Mrs. Elberly's face lighted with relief. "Tom."

"He's pretty hungry. I think you should take him back to Helen's house and feed him," Colin suggested.

Mrs. Elberly's gaze sharpened. "Now don't you try to hoodwink me, Colin Darnell. I've come to see how much damage was done."

For a moment he looked as if he was going to try to dissuade her. Then, as if realizing that would be an exercise in futility, he said, "It's not as bad as it seems at first sight."

The concern on his face and the gentle caring expression in his eyes as he handed Helen the cat, then took hold of Mrs. Elberly's arm, tore at Madaline's heart. She stood watching as he helped the woman toward her house, assuring her firmly that everything could be repaired. Why couldn't he simply be the man she was seeing at this moment?

"Might as well take a look ourselves," Helen said to Madaline.

"Might as well," she replied, forcing herself to remember Colin's other side—a side she could never accept.

"Nearly all of the interior damage is confined to the living room," Colin said as they entered the house. "There's some breakage and the walls and floor in that room got wet. But they're drying well. With a little cleaning and painting this place will look as good as new."

"My pictures," Mrs. Elberly moaned. The table that had stood before the front window was on its side. On the floor nearby were several frames containing photos of the woman's family. The glass in most of the frames was broken.

"You'll cut yourself," Colin cautioned, firming his hold on the elderly woman to prevent her from kneeling and picking up the shattered pieces.

"I'll clean that up and make certain your photographs are cared for," Madaline said, hurrying to Mrs. Elberly's side.

Tears were flooding the woman's eyes. "There's so much damage."

"It can all be repaired," Madaline assured her. She caught the cynical look in Colin's eyes, as if he thought her show of concern was merely an act. Well, she *had* led him to believe she was callous enough to have married for money. Besides, she didn't care what he thought, she told herself again. Her attention returned to the white-haired woman being supported by Colin's arm. "Why don't you go home with Helen now? Tom has had quite a fright. He needs to be fed and you need to rest. This will all look much better by tomorrow."

But Mrs. Elberly's attention had turned to the far side of the room. "My crystals," she said with relief, heading toward a table where several geodes, along with a few singly cut crystals, were on on display. She breathed a sigh of relief. "They're undamaged." Gently she touched a large amethyst-filled geode.

The spires of purple crystal formed a complex design that reminded Madaline of a fairy castle.

"Pretty, isn't it?" the old woman said with a loving smile. "I started collecting these as a child. They're so beautiful. Just looking at them makes me feel good. And sometimes they sing to me. It's so soothing." Her smile was suddenly replaced by a frown. "Except when Chief Brant is here. Then they make a sound like cymbals clashing. It's so loud it hurts my ears." Her face screwed up into a look of discomfort. "And today, they aren't happy.

They're making a shrill sound, like a siren. But who can blame them?"

Tom suddenly let out a yelp of discomfort and, leaping from Helen's arms, darted out of the house.

Mrs. Elberly nodded as if this was to be expected. "You see, I'm not just hearing things. Tom hears them, too." She turned toward Helen. "And don't try to tell me that it's my hearing aid buzzing and that cats have such good hearing Tom can hear it, too."

"I was only going to suggest that Tom's hungry. We should get back to my place and feed him before he runs off to find his own breakfast," Helen said, her voice gently coaxing.

"He's too lazy to fend for himself. He won't go any farther than the front porch," Mrs. Elberly replied as her gaze traveled around the room. The sadness returned to her eyes. "I should stay and help." Still holding on to Colin for support, she moved toward the mantel. Her arthritic hand shook as she righted a small pewter vase.

"Really, I can take care of cleaning up in here," Madaline assured her.

"The doctor said you were to rest today," Helen added, her voice taking on a note of authority. "And he left me to see that you did."

"You can't disobey the doctor's orders," Colin insisted, gently but firmly beginning to guide Mrs. Elberly out of the house.

The old woman came to an abrupt halt. "Are you trying to throw me out of my own home, Colin Darnell?" she demanded.

His gaze leveled on her. "I'm trying to get you someplace safe so I don't have to worry about you while I repair the hole in your roof," he replied honestly.

"Then don't treat me like an addled child. Just tell me to get the hell out of your way," she returned, and began moving toward the door once again.

"Still feisty, aren't you?" he teased.

She laughed lightly, then her expression became serious. "It's going to take me a while to pay you for the repairs," she said. "We'll work out a schedule, though, and you'll get every cent."

Colin shook his head. "This is neighbor helping neighbor," he insisted. "Consider it repayment for all those cherry pies you baked for me when I was a kid."

Mrs. Elberly's smile returned. "You did love my cherry pies," she said reminiscently. She turned toward Helen. "We'd better get out of here and let these people do their work."

As Mrs. Elberly had predicted, Tom was waiting on the front porch. Taking the cat in one arm and aiding Mrs. Elberly with the other, Helen headed toward her home.

Madaline was acutely aware of Colin's presence as they watched the women leave. A disappointment so strong it was like a physical ache swept through her. She wanted to scream at him, tell him how hurt she'd been when she'd discovered the truth. But this wasn't the time or the place. A heaviness on her arm reminded her she was still carrying the basket of food.

"I'll put this in the kitchen," she said, suddenly needing to get away from him. "There are rolls and sandwich fixings in here, as well as a cake. The men can come in and eat whenever they're hungry."

He nodded, then strode outside.

For the rest of the day, Madaline worked on repairing the damage done to the living room. But as hard as she tried, she couldn't keep her mind entirely on her task. She found her attention constantly drawn to Colin. Covertly she studied him. Just watching him filled her with longing. She tried to ignore the feelings, but that was as futile as trying to ignore him.

By five-thirty in the afternoon, Mrs. Elberly's house was well on its way to being repaired—and Madaline's nerves were near the breaking point.

"Let's call it a day and finish tomorrow," she heard Ray Kolby suggest. His words were met with a chorus of agreement.

Madaline wanted to find Colin and vent her long-held anger and disappointment. But when she went outside, he was talking with the men about what they would do the next day. For Devin's sake she didn't dare stand around waiting for Colin; that would cause gossip.

Frustrated, she climbed in her car and left. But instead of driving back to Devin's place, she left town and drove out to Colin's property. Climbing to the ridge, she quickly surveyed the damage that had been done to the foundation work. It didn't look too extensive. But her mind refused to concentrate on it. Instead of making a more thorough inspection, she turned her gaze to a particularly wide surface of exposed flat rock near the edge of the cliff. Without even realizing she was moving, she approached it. Near one end of this wide surface was a boulder. Not a large one; more like a big rock, she thought as she approached it. The top was slightly flattened and the sides rounded. She stopped when she was still a couple of feet away. She knew that the surface on which it now sat was flatter than the top and had a slightly concave shape, like a shallow bowl. A cold chill ran through her.

"You want to tell me why you've been watching me all day?"

Madaline spun around to discover Colin approaching, his expression grim.

Chapter Eight

Madaline's throat felt dry. It occurred to her that maybe she should be afraid. But she was too angry and too frustrated to feel any other emotion. "I was trying to see the real man—the real Colin Darnell."

The insinuation that he was hiding his true self irked Colin. "What you see is what you get."

Madaline glared at him. "I know more about you than you think, Colin Darnell."

He studied her narrowly. There was accusation in her voice. That she had thought she had the right to judge him should have been humorous, he told himself, but he didn't feel like laughing. What he felt was anger. "Just what the hell do you think you know?"

The self-righteous indignation on his face infuriated her even more. "I know about your dark side."

For a long moment Colin stared at her in stunned silence.

Madaline's breath locked in her lungs. He was standing with his feet spread slightly apart and his back straight. It was a fighting stance, and he looked even larger and more intimidating than usual. Maybe being so open hadn't been such a good idea, after all, she thought. A wave of apprehension swept over her.

"What the devil are you talking about?" Colin demanded.

"You know what I'm talking about," she replied, deciding a quick retreat might be best. The urge to run was strong, but she managed a haughty glance to relay the message that she considered this discussion ended, then moved with dignity toward the dirt road.

Colin was confused and he had reached the point of exasperation. She'd haunted him too long for him to let her walk away now, leaving even more unanswered questions between them.

Madaline's heart was pounding with apprehension as she passed him. She'd never seen anyone look as angry as he did. Down deep she couldn't believe that he would actually harm her, but up here on this ridge, the disturbing vision that tormented her dreams was vivid. Suddenly her arm was grasped in a vicelike grip. She couldn't stop a strangled scream from escaping as she jerked around to face him.

Colin glowered down at her. He read the terror in her eyes, and frustration mingled with his anger. Abruptly he released her. "You can't honestly believe I would harm you," he said.

"No," was her gut-level response. *You could be the biggest fool this side of the Mississippi,* her inner voice warned immediately. She took a step back. "Maybe," she hedged. The truth was she just didn't want to believe he would. "I don't know," she confessed.

Colin stared at her. Her retreat hadn't been lost on him. He had told himself that nothing she could do would ever hurt him again. But that little movement had caused a sharp jab of pain. "What did I ever do that would give you any reason to be afraid of me?"

His pure-of-heart routine grated on her. "Don't try to play Mr. Innocent with me, Colin Darnell," she snapped.

The undefined accusations she was hurling at him were growing more annoying by the moment. "Just what do you think you know about me?" he demanded.

Madaline glared at him. He was acting as if he honestly had no idea what she was talking about. But she knew better. "Do you remember that Wednesday in August four years ago? You were supposed to have driven Zebulon into Boston and stayed overnight with him while he had some tests run. He wasn't feeling well, and Dr. James couldn't figure out what was wrong with him."

"I remember." He regarded her grimly. "It was after I got home from that trip that I discovered you'd suddenly decided you never wanted to see me or hear from me again."

She faced him levelly. "That was because I knew you'd never left town. Or if you did drive Zebulon to Boston, you returned here that night and went back to pick him up the next day."

Colin's scowl deepened. "Don't be ridiculous. I drove Zebulon to Boston and I stayed with him. If I hadn't, he'd have bolted and never gone in for the tests." He grimaced as he recalled that night and what had followed. "In fact, I'm not sure if he's really forgiven me for that yet. The tests didn't show anything, and three days later he was right as rain and furious with me for making him stay."

Madaline wanted to scream. *He had everyone fooled.* The entire town thought of him as an honest man, but there he was, standing right in front of her, lying as glibly as a con artist. She could have salvaged some respect for him if he'd just admitted the truth. "I saw you here." She pointed toward the flat rocky surface behind them. "I saw you there!"

Colin studied her. What she was claiming was impossible, but she sure looked as if she believed it. "Why don't you tell me what you saw?" he requested quietly.

Madaline stared at him. Did he think she was so weak-minded he could convince her she hadn't seen what she thought she had? A part of her wished he could, but the images were too vivid. Everything about that night seemed burned into her memory.

"That evening I had dinner with Devin," she said, never taking her eyes off Colin. "By the time we reached dessert, I remember thinking he must be feeling a bit miffed at me. I was having trouble concentrating on our conversation. I'd felt all right when I arrived, but I was starting to feel a little queasy. My mind was hazy and I couldn't stop feeling anxious." A cynical smile played at the corners of her mouth. "I kept thinking about you and wishing I was with you."

Hearing her say those words caused a twisting sensation in his gut. Colin scowled at himself. Whatever had been between them was over.

"Anyway, Devin said he was restless and suggested we go for a drive. I agreed. I thought the fresh air might help clear my mind. We drove past the spot where the stile went over Zebulon's fence. Your truck was parked on the side of the road near it." She paused to give him a chance to confess and save her from having to continue.

An uneasiness swept through Colin. "I left my truck parked in front of Zebulon's place and drove his car to Boston."

This was plausible. Zebulon had a nice car, but he didn't like to drive and rarely went any farther than Smytheshire. Still... "I thought you were going to take the truck so that you could pick up some special building supplies," she challenged.

"I was," he replied, his uneasiness growing stronger. "But when Zebulon and I came out of his place, my truck wouldn't start. I didn't have time to work on it, so we took Zebulon's car."

"Well, it must have gotten fixed on its own because I saw it by the stile that night," she returned.

"Yeah, so you said," he muttered, recalling that when he'd gotten back, he'd discovered that the only problem with the truck had been a couple of loose wires. A cynical look crossed his face. "So you saw my truck, decided I'd lied to you and refused to even speak to me. That was pretty harsh judgment."

"That's not what happened," she retorted, infuriated by his implication that she was that shallow. Abruptly she clamped her mouth shut. Maybe it would have been wiser to let him think that was all she'd seen.

"What did happen?" he demanded.

"I'm sure you can guess." She was furious that he was making her relive the experience by spelling it out for him.

The anger he was feeling etched itself deeply into his features. "I've never been any good at guessing games, Maggie."

His pretense of innocence caused her nerves to snap. "Devin said something about that being a curious place to leave your truck. I couldn't understand why it would be there, either, since I thought you'd driven it into Boston. He pulled over to the side and stopped. That was when he told me about the phone call."

Colin raised an eyebrow. "Phone call?"

"He said that just before I'd arrived at his place for dinner, he'd received a call from someone who didn't identify himself. The anonymous caller had said that if

Devin really considered me a good friend, he should warn me about you. When Devin asked what he was supposed to warn me about, the caller merely said that you hadn't gone into Boston like you'd told me, and if I wanted proof of this, I should take a drive after dark that night out to where the stile crossed old Zebulon's fence."

Madaline drew a shaky breath as the hurt she had felt then assailed her. "Devin said he'd had the impression that the caller was trying to warn me you were two-timing me. He said he hadn't told me about the call during dinner because he didn't want to cause any trouble between us without proof. He said he'd debated all during the meal about coming out here alone to see if the caller was telling the truth. Then he said that, considering how infatuated I was with you, he knew I wouldn't listen to him even if he had proof, so he'd decided to drive me out here. Devin said he'd hoped the caller had been lying."

Madaline paused to swallow the lump that had formed in her throat. "I didn't know what to think," she continued stiffly. "I climbed out of Devin's car and headed for your truck. I was hoping to find a flat tire or some other mechanical problem that would suggest why it was there." A shiver shook her as she remembered what she had found. "Devin followed me. We looked inside. On the front seat was an old book, a really old book. It looked as if it had been written by hand. It was filled with stuff about druid beliefs and ceremonies."

She again paused to give him a chance to confess. This was getting more difficult by the moment, and she really didn't want to continue.

Colin studied her grimly. "Go on," he ordered gruffly.

A shadow flickered in her eyes as she recalled her sense of foreboding as she'd stood by the truck that night. "I was puzzled. I couldn't figure out why you would have a book like that. Devin looked really shaken. He said that maybe the caller wasn't warning us about another woman. He said he'd been reading articles in some of the national magazines about people developing fascinations for some of the ancient religions." The cynical smile returned. "I assured him that you would never get involved with anything like that."

Colin was beginning to get a sick feeling in the pit of his stomach. "I take it you changed your mind."

"*You* changed my mind," she replied. "Devin asked if I had any idea where you might be. I told him about the ridge, but I still refused to consider his suggestion about why you had that book. I figured you were with another woman. I figured you'd gotten bored with me and wanted a little variety. I didn't want to go up there, but I needed to see for myself. I kept hoping all during the climb that I was wrong." She stopped as the memory of what they'd found filled her mind. "I almost wish it had been another woman," she admitted in a voice barely above a whisper.

"And what did you see when you got there?" he asked, certain he wasn't going to like what he was about to hear, but needing to hear it.

"We saw you. You were dressed in a long brown monk's robe with the hood up over your head. That rock—" she pointed toward the smaller boulder she had been staring at earlier "—had been rolled into the center of that flat area, and several smaller rocks had been placed in a wide circle around it. A small fire had been built on top of the center rock. While we watched, you took a rabbit out of a trap by the edge of the circle of rocks. Then, while you chanted something, you killed it and laid it on the fire." Her stomach churned. She recalled that the queasiness she'd been feeling during dinner had grown stronger, and she'd come very close to throwing up at that point. "I can still remember the smell."

Colin was studying her narrowly. "You saw my face?"

"No," she admitted. "The hood was pulled fairly far down and it was dark." She remembered having to squint hard to keep her eyes focused. "But I recognized the knife. It was your hunting knife. The one with the carved wooden handle."

"You saw my truck and a knife that looked like mine and condemned me on that evidence?"

Madaline stared at him. All these years she'd been so certain it was him. Now a shadow of doubt began to creep into her mind. "Are you claiming it wasn't you?"

"I was in Boston." Contempt laced his voice. "You never even gave me a chance to defend myself."

He was right, she admitted. But at the time she hadn't had the nerve to face him. "I was shocked and frightened," she said.

Then her back stiffened. He could be lying. If what she'd believed all these years was true, then she should expect him to try to lie his way out of it.

"Maybe you were just looking for an excuse to be rid of me," he suggested dryly. "Maybe it had occurred to you how much you would be giving up if you chose me over Devin."

She knew she'd given him reason to think that, but it still hurt. "That's not true." She was certain her denial fell on deaf ears, but she had to say it anyway.

"If you really believe it was me, then shouldn't you be frightened right now?" he challenged scornfully.

"I suppose," she conceded. Frustration welled within her. "I never wanted to believe it was you," she heard herself confess. "But all of the evidence pointed to you. There was your truck, your knife and the fact that this ridge was your private spot. And I remembered how pleased you were when I christened it Sanctuary Ridge, as if that was the perfect name for it."

Colin saw the uncertainty in her eyes. "And despite my denial, you still think it was me, don't you?" he asked, the bitterness he was feeling reflected in his voice.

"I don't know. I want to believe you," she said shakily. Tears of frustration burned at the back of her eyes. "The problem is that I want to believe you too much. I cared about you." She still cared, she realized, but pride refused to allow her to tell him that. "Four years ago, I was afraid of being fooled by you. I wanted so much to believe you could never possess such a cruel side I was afraid I would swallow any lie you told. I guess I'm still afraid of that."

Her words cut like a knife. "How can you claim to have honestly cared about someone you have so little trust in?" Unable to face her, he stalked off toward the path that worked its way down the side of the mountain to the lake and on to Zebulon's house.

Madaline watched him disappear into the woods. The hooded figure hadn't been him. She knew that now. No matter what the evidence was she believed him. She was also just as certain that he would never forgive her for not trusting him. The urge to cry was strong. Her gaze shifted to the wide flat rock surface where she'd seen the monk-like figure. "I was just so terribly frightened," she said quietly in her defense, recalling the terror that had filled her that night. She'd felt sick for several days afterward and for weeks she'd awoken nearly every night in a cold sweat from nightmares about the incident. Even now the memory caused a feeling of nausea and fear. She turned away and started down the dirt road toward her car.

By the time Colin reached the lake, his anger hadn't diminished. That Maggie could believe he had such a barbarous side caused him raw pain. How could he have cared about a woman who thought so little of him? he wondered as he stared out over the water.

His jaw tensed as he looked up toward the ridge. Someone had made that phone call four years ago, and most likely that same someone had played the part of the hooded figure. "And that person went to a lot of trouble to make it look as if he was me," he muttered. Now Maggie was getting weird phone calls and unsettling notes. Concern for her swept over him. That he still could feel so much for her irritated him. *I'd feel the same for anyone I thought might be in danger,* he told himself. Besides, this was different. He'd been included in the perpetrator's game, and he didn't like being used.

Madaline felt as though the world were closing in on her as she turned into Devin's drive. The feeling of being caged grew even stronger as she parked.

"I was just getting ready to go looking for you," Devin said, coming out to meet her. "I called Mrs. Elberly's place. Helen Ashbey answered. She said the only reason she was there was that Mrs. Elberly had insisted on going over to see what repairs had been done so far. She said all the workers had left over an hour ago."

Madaline experienced a wave of guilt for causing the look of concern on his face. This was quickly followed by irritation. *He's worse than an overprotective parent,* she thought, then chided herself for this. He'd always been there for her when she needed help, and she should be grateful to him.

"I drove out to see for myself how much damage had been done to the foundation of Colin's house," she replied. "I didn't mean to worry you."

He slipped an arm around her shoulders as he accompanied her toward the front door. "You look upset. Was it extensive? I know you want to get his job finished as quickly as possible."

Madaline shook her head. "The damage wasn't bad. It shouldn't cause more than a couple of days' delay."

Devin continued to regard her anxiously. "Then why do you look so shaken?"

"Colin showed up." Madaline raked a hand through her hair. "I told him about that night—about seeing the hooded figure on the ridge."

Devin looked horrified. "You should be more careful. A man who practices druid rites isn't one you should trust."

"He says it wasn't him."

Devin cocked an eyebrow. "You sound as if you believe him."

"I do believe him," she replied.

"If I remember correctly, one of your reasons for not confronting him years ago was that you were afraid he might be able to talk you into believing whatever he wanted," he reminded her.

"I know." Her jaw firmed. "But I just know it wasn't him."

"You're still in love with him," Devin said with a disapproving shake of his head. He studied her worriedly. "And how does he feel about you?"

"He despises me."

Devin gave her shoulder a brotherly squeeze. "Maybe that's for the best. You may trust him, but I don't. I'd swear it was him in that hooded robe on the ridge."

Madaline shook off his hold and turned to face him squarely. "You're not being fair. Neither of us was fair to Colin." Challenge flashed in her eyes. "Did you see his face that night?"

Devin hesitated, his expression one of deep thought. Finally he shook his head. "No," he admitted. Catching her chin, he looked pleadingly down at her. "Don't be angry with me. I'm only concerned about your welfare."

"I wish you wouldn't worry about me so much," she said tiredly.

He slipped his arm around her shoulders again and gently guided her into the house. "I'm sure everything will work out just fine," he said soothingly. "And I'm sure Colin doesn't really despise you."

"And I'm sure he does," she replied, then wished she'd kept her mouth shut when she noticed Mrs. Grayson standing in the entrance hall. From the look on the woman's face she knew the housekeeper had heard this last exchange.

Giving proof to this assumption, Mrs. Grayson said sternly, "If you ask me, you should stay away from that man."

Devin frowned. "Colin is an old friend of Madaline's."

"More like an old enemy, if you want my opinion," the housekeeper replied. Her gaze focused on Madaline. "I recall you and Colin Darnell were an item once, then you broke it off. There are stories in the paper nearly everyday about a boyfriend killing the girl who jilted him."

Madaline glared at the woman. "Colin Darnell would never harm me or anyone," she said with conviction.

"That's what all the neighbors say on the news when they're interviewed about the man who lived next door and has just been arrested for murder," Mrs. Grayson returned warningly.

"I won't have Colin Darnell spoken about that way," Madaline retorted.

Devin's hold around her shoulders tightened protectively. "Mrs. Grayson, you're upsetting my wife. I'm sure your analogy is quite uncalled for."

The housekeeper frowned. "I just wouldn't want to see anything horrible happen to either of you," she said.

"Nothing horrible is going to happen to either of us unless dinner is late," Devin replied. "We're both close to starving to death. Will you please go check with Claire to see if everything is on time?"

"Every meal in this house is *always* on time." Mrs. Grayson continued to frown at them as if they were being unreasonably stubborn.

"Check, anyway," Devin ordered.

For a moment she looked as if she was going to protest, then she started down the hall. But before she'd gone more than two steps, she turned back. "You'd be wise to heed my warning," she said curtly, then continued toward the kitchen.

As soon as she was gone, Devin turned to Madaline. "I don't know what's gotten into that woman," he said apologetically. "Please don't be upset with her. She means well."

"I don't like her talking about Colin that way," Madaline said. "It isn't fair."

The concern on Devin's face increased. "Are you certain you're not allowing your emotions to rule your reason?"

Madaline turned toward him. "Yes," she said with conviction.

For a moment Devin looked as if he was going to try to dissuade her, then he smiled indulgently. "You've always had a stubborn streak and a loyalty I admire, even though I'm afraid it might be misplaced in this instance." With a sympathetic expression that let her know he was sure she was allowing herself to be fooled, he added, "Why don't you run along and have a nice hot shower before dinner? It might help you relax a little."

Madaline nodded. A shower sounded good. Being alone sounded even better. Devin's indulgent manner was getting on her nerves. She resented being treated like a child whose judgment was questionable. As she ascended the stairs, she glanced over her shoulder to discover him watching her with an anxious frown. *He's just worried about me,* she reminded herself. *I should be glad to have him in the role of my big brother.* She felt guilty for being irritated by him, but as she continued up the stairs, the walls of the house felt as if they were closing in on her.

Chapter Nine

"I want to start divorce proceedings as soon after your birthday as possible," Madaline said. To insure their privacy, she had waited until they had finished eating dinner and Devin had gone into his library. Then she had followed him.

Devin replaced the book he had been taking down from a high shelf when she entered. "I noticed you didn't eat much dinner," he said as he climbed down from the ornately carved cherrywood ladder. Approaching her, he took her hand in his. "Your freedom is yours for the asking. That was our agreement. ' He regarded her speculatively. "Have you decided to fight for Colin's love?"

Madaline breathed a heavy sigh. "I doubt I could win it."

Devin smiled encouragingly. "I'm sure you could." The smile was replaced by a worried frown. "But I'm not so sure it would be best for you." He held up his hand to stave off her objection. "I know you're angry with me for saying that, but I'm not convinced Colin is safe. People believe what they want to believe. *You* want to believe him when he says he wasn't the hooded figure, but I'm not convinced."

Madaline knew he was being logical, but she still felt angry with him. Before she could respond in Colin's defense, a knock interrupted.

"Enter," Devin called out.

"He's here." Mrs. Grayson looked and sounded as if she were announcing the arrival of the devil himself.

Madaline knew immediately who the woman meant, and her temper flared at the housekeeper's attitude.

"Who's here?" Devin asked, his manner implying that he knew of no one who would warrant such a reaction from Mrs. Grayson.

"Colin Darnell," Mrs. Grayson replied with stiff formality, an expression of disapproval on her face.

"Show him in," Devin directed.

Mrs. Grayson gave a shrug as if to say she'd done her best to warn them. "Yes, sir."

A few moments later Colin entered.

It was curious, Madaline thought. She'd always disliked this room. It was too closed in, too dark for her taste. But with Colin there, the atmosphere suddenly seemed brighter. The hope that he had come to tell her that he'd forgiven her filled her. But it did not last more than a moment. When he looked at her there was ice in his eyes, and once again an aloneness swept over her.

Crossing the room, Devin closed the door to assure their privacy. Turning to Colin, he said evenly, "Madaline has been telling me that you've assured her you were not the hooded figure we saw that night."

"I wasn't." Colin heard the edge of doubt in Devin's voice and it angered him. But he had promised himself he would not lose his temper. He would simply say what he'd come to say and leave. "I've been trying to figure out why someone would set me up like that. It could have been someone wanting to get even, but I can't think of anyone I could have made that mad, except for Harvey Clark, and he didn't have the brains to set something like that up. He was more of the type to jump out of the bushes and attack an unsuspecting passerby. That leaves someone who wanted to break me and Maggie up. If that's the case, you're my number-one suspect." A cynical expression came over his face. "You could have saved yourself a lot of trouble. She would have come back to you, anyway."

Madaline started to protest, then swallowed her words. They would be useless and she had her pride.

"I do not play childish games," Devin said frostily.

Colin frowned. "Didn't sound childish to me. Slaughtering an animal and pretending to offer it in sacrifice sounds demented."

"If you're accusing me of something, just say it," Devin ordered curtly.

During his drive here, Colin had been remembering the time Devin had kicked the puppy. It didn't seem all that farfetched to believe the man might hire someone to slaughter a small animal and pretend to offer it for sacrifice. Still, he wasn't quite ready to make that accusation.

Madaline watched the two men squaring off. What Colin was suggesting didn't make any sense. Admittedly, in the beginning, Devin had been dubious about her dating Colin, but he had accepted her growing feelings for the man. He'd even been happy to see *her* so happy.

"Devin would never do such a thing," she said, attempting to calm the situation.

Colin turned toward her, Devin momentarily forgotten. "There was a time when I thought you'd come to my defense that quickly," he said, his voice laced with accusation. Immediately he berated himself. She'd made her choice and he told himself he should be glad she hadn't chosen him. A woman with such a cold heart she'd marry for money and then proudly admit to it was not someone with whom he wanted to share his life.

Madaline felt as if she'd been punched in the stomach. But she could not fault him or defend herself against the contempt she read in his eyes. She should have had more faith in him.

Colin saw the sudden look of remorse on her face. It tore at his resolve. *Don't play the fool for her again,* he warned himself.

He jerked his attention back to Devin. "If you were involved with the incident on the ridge, it doesn't matter to me. I just want to make it clear that I wasn't the hooded person you two saw. And if you did have something to do with that little scene, then these phone calls and letters Maggie..." he paused and corrected himself "... Mrs. Smythe and I have been getting are not related to it, because you sure as heck wouldn't have wanted me back here, and you sure wouldn't be bringing up her virginity. But if you had nothing to do with the incident on the ridge, then whoever did arrange it is very likely the one making the phone calls and sending the notes. In that case, I'd say you have a possible nut on your hands and you'd better guard your wife."

There, he'd said what he came to say. Turning abruptly, he stalked out of the room.

Madaline stood rigid, listening to his footsteps as they echoed down the hall. Colin despised her, and yet he'd come to make certain Devin protected her...

"If that wasn't Colin on the ridge that night, then it could have been someone's idea of a practical joke—a very bad one," Devin said, breaking the silence that had descended over the room. "And if it was, the notes and phone calls could be another tasteless joke. On the other hand, Colin could be right. There might be someone in this town who is a bit unbalanced. In which case that person has been keeping a very close eye on both of us, especially you. Perhaps it would be a good idea for me to stick close to you for a while."

"You can't possibly follow me around like a shadow," she protested.

Devin placed an arm around her shoulders. "It's a husband's duty to protect his wife, and I do try to be the best husband I can."

"You've been a fine husband," Madaline assured him. "But I can't live my life under constant guard."

"Not your whole life, just until we can resolve this matter," Devin insisted.

Madaline frowned. "I really haven't been threatened," she pointed out again. Her frown deepened. "I think there's someone in this town who enjoys playing elaborate practical jokes. He's probably played them on others, but nobody's talking because the jokes are cruel and personal."

"There are people with warped senses of humor." Devin's jaw formed a resolute line. "But I'm still going to be your constant companion until I'm satisfied you're not in any danger."

Madaline could see that arguing would be useless. Besides, he might be right. A bit of precaution wouldn't hurt. "I could use some help," she said. "I have to repaint Mrs. Elberly's living room tomorrow."

"Sounds like fun," Devin replied.

Fun. That word seemed so out of place in this room, Madaline thought, realizing the dreary stifling atmosphere had returned. She forced a yawn. "I'm exhausted. I think I'll go to bed."

Devin gave her a hug. "You're very precious to me,

Madaline. I intend to see you achieve the destiny you deserve," he promised, placing a light kiss on her forehead.

The destiny I want is to spend the rest of my life with Colin Darnell, she admitted to herself as she bid him goodnight and left. But that was one destiny that would never be hers.

"Mrs. Smythe, could I speak to you for a moment?"

Madaline was startled. She had been so wrapped up in her inner thoughts, she hadn't noticed the housekeeper standing in the hall. At the moment, she wasn't interested in talking to anyone. But politeness refused to allow her to tell the woman that. "Yes, of course."

"In the conservatory," the woman suggested.

Madaline nodded. At least Mrs. Grayson had chosen pleasant surroundings, she mused, as she followed the housekeeper to the other wing. But tonight as she entered the glass enclosure, even the greeting issued by the sweet scents of the flowers and plants didn't lighten her mood.

Mrs. Grayson waited until the door was closed, then said, "I don't know what's going on between you and Mr. Devin and Colin Darnell, but I do know that I don't want to see Mr. Devin hurt. I remember four years ago when you began seeing Colin Darnell. Mr. Devin never said anything against the man, but I could see he wasn't pleased." Mrs. Grayson sighed wistfully. "He loves you very much."

"I love him, too," Madaline assured the woman. And she did love him, like a brother.

Mrs. Grayson smiled. "I'm so glad to hear that. My husband and I never had any children of our own. I guess I sort of think of Mr. Devin as a son. I'd do anything in my power to assure his happiness." She approached Madaline and took her hand. "Your being here has made him very happy. I wouldn't want to see Colin Darnell spoil that."

Madaline knew Mrs. Grayson thought highly of Devin. She had not, however, been aware of the woman's intense loyalty to him. For a brief moment, she considered the possibility that Mrs. Grayson had played out the role of the hooded figure, then discounted that as truly absurd. The woman was too short, hated killing even insects and was genuinely religious. She would never, even in a mock ceremony, perform a pagan ritual.

"Colin is not going to come between Devin and me," she assured the housekeeper.

Mrs. Grayson's smile brightened. "I'm so relieved to hear that."

Even in this, her favorite room, Madaline experienced the sensation of being caught in a trap. Suddenly she felt utterly exhausted. "It's been a long day," she said. "If you'll excuse me, I was on my way to bed."

Escaping to the privacy of her room, she changed into her nightgown. But she was too tense to sleep. Colin's image taunted her. He had every right to dislike her. She had treated him unfairly. With every fiber of her being, she regretted not having faced him four years ago.

She frowned at her image in the mirror. That kind of cowardliness was not like her. But she had been so terribly frightened. That touch of the flu—or whatever it was that had made her feel ill for a few days—hadn't helped, either. It had kept her mind fuzzy, weakened her will and allowed her uneasiness to grow stronger. "There's no sense in making excuses for myself," she said tiredly. "What's done is done and can't be undone."

A knock on her door made her jump.

"I thought you might like a little hot chocolate," Devin said when she answered and found him standing there.

She looked at the tray he was carrying. It was set with two cups, a bowl of small marshmallows, a silver teapot from which wafted the scent of warm chocolate and a plate of small chocolate cakes. All her favorite indulgences. Normally she would have been grateful for his effort to cheer her up, but tonight she would have preferred to be alone. Still, she forced a smile. "You're going to spoil me."

"You deserve a bit of spoiling," he replied, carrying the tray to the small round mahogany table in front of the window. "I know the past couple of weeks have been difficult."

Madaline followed him and sank into one of the two Queen Anne chairs that flanked the table. He couldn't possibly know *how* difficult, she thought, but she kept it to herself. "How are your experiments coming?" she asked, turning the conversation in another direction.

"It's hard to say," he replied. "I'm really just a dabbler." Picking up the cup of hot chocolate she'd just poured for him, he took a sip, then proceeded to explain his latest project in minute detail.

Madaline drank her chocolate while she listened. She tried to concentrate on what he was saying, but her mind began to drift. She felt foggy, vacant. *I must be even more exhausted than I thought,* she mused as she fought to follow his words.

"You look exhausted, and here I am rattling on and on," Devin said apologetically. Setting his barely touched cup aside, he regarded her worriedly. "The truth is, I've been avoiding what I really came up here to say."

Madaline breathed a tired sigh and tried to focus on what he was saying. She knew he was going to bring up Colin again.

"I still can't convince myself that you should trust Colin Darnell," Devin said. "It occurred to me that he could have sent himself that letter and made that phone call to you, as well as sent you the note you received—just to stir up trouble. After all, you did jilt him. He could have somehow found out about my problem and decided to use it to cause us grief. We only have his word that he wasn't the hooded figure."

A part of Madaline's mind couldn't fault Devin's logic. A feeling of fear threatened to overwhelm her. Then Colin's image filled her mind. "No, he would not torture us, and I believe him when he says he was not on the ridge that night," she said as firmly as her growing exhaustion would allow.

"He could have another reason other than to simply torture us," Devin persisted. "He could have found out about my problem and devised this scheme to frighten you into having an affair with him. Then he could be planning to dump you. That would satisfy his male ego and get even with you at the same time."

Madaline scowled. "I will not believe he would even consider something so cruel." A dryness entered her voice. "And I can absolutely assure you that having an affair with me is the last thing Colin is interested in."

Devin regarded her thoughtfully. "I still can't help thinking the man is dangerous."

Again a rush of fear swept through her. She closed her eyes and Colin's image filled her mind once more. She saw him helping old Mrs. Elberly. "The only thing dangerous about Colin Darnell is the threat he poses to my peace of mind," she replied.

Devin rose. Leaning forward he kissed her lightly on the tip of her nose. "For your sake, I hope you're right," he said. "Now let me help you into bed. I don't think I've ever seen you this tired."

Madaline started to tell him that his aid was unnecessary, but when she tried to rise, her legs felt like lead weights. "Thanks," she said.

Devin tucked her in, and she was asleep before he had even left the room.

Chapter Ten

Madaline awoke the next morning with a pounding headache, accompanied by an underlying apprehensiveness. A couple of aspirin eased the throbbing in her head, and Devin's enthusiasm for painting Mrs. Elberly's living room lightened her mood. As they pulled up in front of the woman's home, they discovered Colin's truck already there.

Madaline immediately found herself searching him out. He was on the roof. She saw him glance over his shoulder at her and Devin, but he didn't wave. He simply turned his attention back to the job at hand, as if their presence was too insignificant to acknowledge.

"I really think it's for the best if he keeps his distance," Devin said in her ear, obviously noticing Colin's unenthusiastic welcome.

Again Madaline found herself feeling irritated with Devin. She also had a strong urge to climb onto the roof with

Colin and beg him to forgive her. But she knew he wouldn't.

"Come along," Devin said, pulling her attention back to him. "I'm dying to learn how to paint."

"You won't be saying that tomorrow when you wake up with a sore arm and a stiff neck," she warned him. Forcing herself not to look at Colin again, she opened the trunk and began taking out painting supplies.

Covertly Colin watched them enter the house. He was relieved to see that Devin was taking this business about the letters more seriously and not letting Maggie go running around on her own. Now maybe he could get some rest. He'd called himself a fool a hundred times during the night. When he'd first gone to bed, he hadn't been able to sleep. He had finally dozed off only to be awakened by a terrifying nightmare in which Maggie was being stalked by a hooded figure. Colin had tried to save her but he'd been too late. After that, he'd laid awake for hours trying to figure out who could be playing this game with him and Maggie—and why. It's probably just someone with a really warped sense of humor, he decided as he fitted a shingle into place.

Recalling that the letter he'd received had merely said Maggie could use a little help from a friend and that none of her messages had carried a real threat, he told himself maybe the whole thing was just a tempest in a teapot. Nothing was going to happen. He'd been a fool to come back here.

Something large and furry suddenly brushed his arm. Startled, he jerked away, scraping his hand on a rough edge of a shingle. "Damn," he cursed. As Mrs. Elberly's cat scurried away, he looked down to discover blood running from the jagged cut and muttered, "That should teach me to keep my mind on my work."

For a long moment, he considered not doing anything about the wound, but the blood was flowing fairly heavily. *I'd be stupid to let myself get an infection just because I don't want to be in the same house with them,* he admonished himself. Grudgingly he made his way down the ladder.

After instructing Devin to stir the paint, Madaline had gone into the kitchen to start brewing a pot of coffee for the workers. Hearing the approach of booted footsteps, she assumed it was one of the Kolbys and turned smilingly to greet him. But the smile on her face vanished as Colin entered. Then she saw his bloody hand and her heart caught in her throat.

"I'll drive you to the doctor," she said, forgetting about the coffee and Devin, thinking only of Colin.

Colin found himself wanting to believe that the concern in her eyes was deeper than a mere surface reaction to the sight of blood. But he'd already allowed his feelings to make a fool of him once; he wouldn't do that again.

"It's not as bad as it looks," he said, quickly turning away from her and heading toward the sink. "It just needs to be washed and bandaged."

"I've got a first-aid kit in the car." Madaline was already on her way out of the kitchen before the sentence was even finished. Jogging to the car, she hoped he was right. If he wasn't, she'd make him go see the doctor. She noticed that her hands were shaking as she opened the trunk and took out the kit.

"What's going on?" Devin asked, coming out of the living room as she reentered the house.

"Colin hurt his hand," she replied, forcing a calmness into her voice she didn't feel.

"Badly?" Devin asked, falling into step behind her as she hurried to the kitchen.

In spite of his distrust of Colin, Madaline noted Devin's concern seemed truly honest. "He says not. But all I could see was blood." She'd reached the kitchen. Colin was standing by the sink. He'd lathered his hands with soap and was now rinsing them. There was a grim set to his jaw that told her his wound was causing him pain. "How does it look?" she asked as she approached him.

Colin dried his hands, then frowned at the injured palm. The gash was still bleeding but it wasn't deep. "It's nothing, more of a scrape than a cut," he replied. He turned and saw Devin in the doorway. *He's protecting her from me,* he thought acidly. *Well, there's no need. I've got no designs on her.*

Madaline frowned down at his hand. "It looks painful," she said, her chin threatening to tremble.

The catch in her voice caused Colin's stomach to knot. He wanted her to care. He wanted it so badly it was painful. Don't let her fool you again, he ordered himself. "I've had worse," he said gruffly, reaching for the medical kit.

"You can't bandage your own hand. I'll do it," she insisted, putting the kit on the counter. It didn't matter to her that he despised her. She was determined to make sure his injury was properly cared for.

Colin considered refusing. But she was right. He couldn't bandage his own hand as well as she could. Besides, he didn't want her to guess how much her close proximity was affecting him. And it was definitely affecting him. Her hair was pulled back by a bandanna and her head was turned away from him as she went through the first-aid kit, taking out what she wanted. In that position, he had a clear view of her ear. There was a hollow behind that ear that he used to like to kiss just to hear her playful giggle. He turned his attention back to his hand.

Madaline had found an antiseptic cream. "I'm going to put some of this on before I wrap your hand," she said.

She'd been trying to concentrate on the kit and his wound, but his nearness was making that difficult. His after-shave was playing havoc with her senses. And even though he was not touching her, every fiber of her being was as aware of him as if she was being held in his arms. Bandage his wound, she ordered herself, and get out of here. She picked up a sterile pad and placed her free hand under his injured one as she began to blot the blood still flowing from the cut.

Colin clamped his jaw shut to hold back a gasp. The feel of her hand cradling his own caused a searing heat to travel up his arm.

"It looks as if the bleeding is stopping," Madaline said, marveling that she had put together a coherent sentence. She'd thought she couldn't feel more shaken. Then she'd taken his hand in hers and a fire had ignited down deep inside. Sternly she ordered herself not to think of the strength of his hand or how exciting it would feel to be caressed by it.

"Figured it wouldn't bleed long," he replied, fighting down the urge to run his free hand along the curves of her body. He could still remember how deliciously intoxicated he would feel when she trembled slightly and her eyes flamed with passion. *Too bad we were so damned innocent,* he thought wryly. Maybe if they had been intimate, this hold she had over him wouldn't be so strong. Maybe then he'd know that she couldn't make him feel any more pleasure than any other woman.

His breath was warm and inviting against her skin. Madaline laid the pad aside and squeezed out some of the ointment into his palm. As she carefully smeared the cream along the line of the cut, her fingers brushed against the rough callused surface, and currents of heat raced from her fingertips to the very core of her being.

Colin had been so certain he had steeled himself against her. But although her touch was featherlight, it was kindling a passion so strong his control was being seriously threatened. His gaze shifted to her face. Her attention, he noted, was focused on his wound.

Madaline had the most tremendous urge to kiss his hand. But not with a kiss-and-make-it-better kiss. Recalling how she had once playfully tasted the tips of his fingers and discovered they were mildly salty, she wondered if they would taste the same today. This thought fueled the fire within her until it felt like a raging inferno. Her tongue came out to wet her suddenly dry lips.

Watching her, Colin could almost taste the moist warmth of her mouth. He wanted to feel the length of her pressed tightly against him and claim her lips to see if they were as sweet as he remembered.

Madaline didn't want to look up at him, but she couldn't stop herself. She expected to see contempt carved into his features. Instead, she saw her own passion mirrored in his eyes. Her heart seemed to pause for a moment, then it began pounding wildly. Her lips moved, forming his name in a silent question.

When she looked at him that way, he couldn't think. He drew a shaky breath. Any second now he was going to kiss her, and nothing in this world could stop him—

"Guess the Kolbys are going to have to finish the roof by themselves," Devin said from the doorway.

Colin froze. He'd been wrong. Reality, in the form of her rich husband, had stopped him, saving him from making a complete fool of himself.

Madaline saw the ice crystallize in Colin's eyes. The contempt she'd expected to see a moment earlier now showed on his face, along with a look of self-disgust. Bile rose in her throat. He might still feel a physical attraction to her, but he hated himself for it. Abruptly she returned her attention to bandaging his hand.

"I'll be able to finish the job," Colin responded coolly to Devin's remark. "I sent the Kolbys up to the ridge to work on my house." He disliked admitting even to himself that he'd chosen to finish Mrs. Elberly's house, instead of having one of the brothers do it, so that he could keep an eye on Maggie and make certain she was safe. She didn't need his protection. She had Devin's.

Madaline wanted to run from the room, find a dark corner and have a good cry. But she knew that crying wouldn't do any good. Instead, she finished binding the bandage and said stiffly, "You should wear some gloves to protect the bandage and make certain you don't get the wound dirty." A sudden sense of relief came over her as an avenue of escape presented itself. "I'll make a quick trip to Johnson's Hardware store and get some."

Colin studied her. For a moment, just before she'd lowered her gaze, he could have sworn she looked as if she wanted to cry. And right now, although she was hiding it well, he could tell she was shaken. The thought that she might be regretting having married Devin crossed his mind. But that didn't change the fact that she'd married the man for his money. Still, he wished she didn't look so vulnerable. Because she isn't, he told himself. Inside she was hard as nails. But at that moment, as she continued to avoid looking at him, he was having some trouble believing that. She's made her choice, he told himself curtly.

Madaline closed the first-aid kit. "I'll be back in a few minutes," she said, starting toward the door.

"There's no need for you to go to Johnson's." Colin had been going to say he had a pair of gloves in his truck, but as he turned and saw her and Devin, a sharp jab of pain shot through him. "This hand is bothering me more than I thought it would," he lied. "I'm going to drive up to the ridge and send the Kolbys back to finish this job. With both of them working, they can have it done by noon. Then if you two need help with the painting, they can lend you a hand."

Before either Devin or Madaline could respond, he brushed past Devin and strode out of the house.

"Are you all right?" Devin asked.

Madaline blinked to bring her eyes back in focus. Even though Devin had been standing right there, she'd barely been aware of his presence as she'd watched Colin leave. "Yes, I'm fine," she lied.

Devin smiled encouragingly. "Then how about if you finish with that coffee and I finish stirring the paint."

Madaline nodded and quickly turned toward the counter. Hot tears were burning at the back of her eyes and she wasn't certain a few weren't going to escape. To her chagrin, they did as Devin started back into the living room. As she brushed them away, she wondered if it would make any difference if she told Colin why she'd wanted Devin's money. It might, but there was still the matter of her lack of trust in him. She doubted that he'd ever forgive her for that. She breathed a tired sigh. When her obligation to Devin was over, she was going to leave Smytheshire. She didn't know where she would go, but it would be far away from here.

Chapter Eleven

Madaline awoke the next morning with another monstrous headache. ‘‘I’m going to have to give up drinking hot chocolate before I go to bed,’’ she told Devin as they sat eating breakfast.

He glanced at her with a questioning frown. ‘‘I thought you enjoyed it.’’

A rush of guilt swept over her. He’d brought her hot chocolate again last night and it had relaxed her. Now she was suggesting that his thoughtfulness was causing her to feel ill. ‘‘I do,’’ she replied quickly. ‘‘I’m sure this headache is just from the paint fumes.’’

Devin’s frown deepened. ‘‘Or maybe it’s because of Colin Darnell.’’

‘‘Maybe,’’ Madaline admitted. Colin had been on her mind when she’d gone to sleep, and although her dreams were hazy, she knew he’d been in them.

‘‘That man could give anyone a headache.’’

Madaline twisted around to discover that Mrs. Grayson had entered the room. It irritated her that Devin had brought up Colin in the woman's presence. But then, he probably hadn't noticed the housekeeper's entrance either, she guessed. The thought that maybe they should hang a bell around Mrs. Grayson's neck occurred to her. *This headache is making me very grouchy,* she admonished herself. Aloud she said calmly, "I'm sure it was the paint fumes."

"And what are our plans for today?" Devin asked, pointedly changing the subject.

"I need to work on the design for the office complex in Greenfield," Madaline answered, then grimaced as she added, "And this afternoon, we have to go by Mrs. Elberly's for tea. Helen called me last night. Several of the women from church were at Mrs. Elberly's until late last evening. They were putting the living room back in order after the paint dried, so that Mrs. Elberly could move back in last night. Now, she's insisting on having everyone who worked on her home over to thank them."

Madaline had to admit that she really didn't mind going to the tea. It was the prospect of seeing Colin that had her nerves on edge. She'd come close to making a fool of herself yesterday. But even while a part of her wasn't anxious to face him, another part longed for the sight of him. *He's making me crazy,* she thought.

"Can you work on the plans here or do we need to go to your office?" Devin asked as soon as Mrs. Grayson had left.

"I was going to work in my office. But you needn't come. Samantha will be there."

"Where you go, I go," Devin declared.

Madaline frowned into her coffee as the feeling of being caged once again assailed her "I hate being a nuisance to you," she said.

Devin reached over and gave her hand a squeeze. "You're not a nuisance. I was merely planning to do some reading this morning. I can do that in your office as easily as here."

When Mrs. Grayson returned, he instructed her to have Claire pack them a picnic lunch. "I'm going to spend the day with my wife," he informed her.

The housekeeper smiled brightly. "Married couples should spend time together," she said with approval.

But having a husband hovering over a wife can get on the wife's nerves very quickly, Madaline decided a couple of hours later. She was seated at her drawing board. Devin was across the room in one of the large upholstered chairs, reading and drinking coffee. The atmosphere in the room should have been relaxed and his presence should have been a comfort to her. But instead, he made her feel confined and nervous.

Setting aside her pencil, she turned toward him. "This is not going to work."

"Are you having trouble with your design?" he asked, setting aside his book.

"No, it's not the design. It's you spending your days tagging along with me." He looked hurt and she quickly added, "It's not fair to you." Then honesty made her admit, "And being guarded so closely makes me uneasy."

"It's supposed to make you feel safe," he replied, a hint of impatience creeping into his voice.

Devin rarely showed impatience with her. But the last couple of weeks had to have been difficult for him, too, she realized. The fear of being exposed had to be a strain on him, and she again felt guilty for causing him any distress.

"It does," she said. *Liar,* her little voice returned. He was right. She should feel safe, but the truth was she felt as if she was being guarded rather than protected. "I also feel guilty,'' she hedged, attempting to give him a reason for not wanting him hovering over her that would not hurt his feelings. "No matter how much you say it isn't so, I know I'm taking you away from your plants and your experiments, and you're going to start resenting me for it.''

Devin sighed. "You're right,'' he admitted.

Madaline drew a breath of relief. She'd known he had to feel that way. That explained why there was so much tension in the room.

''I've been thinking about hiring a private investigator,'' he continued. ''Maybe they can find out who this prankster is. And if they think this business merits you having a full-time bodyguard, then I'll hire one. I don't care what the town thinks or if my secret gets out. Your safety is what's most important to me. But it will take me a week or so to arrange things.''

Madaline wasn't thrilled with the idea of a bodyguard, but she was pleased by the idea of finding out who was sending the letters.

''In the meantime, however, I must insist that you put up with my company,'' Devin finished.

Madaline nodded. "I've never minded your company,'' she assured him. *At least not until lately,* she added to herself.

''I'll speak to Colin at the tea this afternoon,'' Devin continued thoughtfully. ''I'll need his letter to go along with the one you received. I'm sure whoever I hire will want to see everything.''

The tea loomed in Madaline's mind as she returned her attention to the drawing board. She wondered if Colin would actually be there. Just the thought of him caused a hard knot of aching within her. Remembering his wound, she hoped he'd taken care of his hand properly and that it was healing. When her eyes focused on the paper in front of her again, she discovered she'd written his name. It had been pride that had made her let him think she had married Devin for purely mercenary reasons. As soon as she had the opportunity, she would tell him the truth. But she doubted that would make any difference. Her lack of trust would be what mattered the most to him. But at least he would not think quite so badly of her.

Ever since she and Devin had arrived at the tea, Madaline had been surreptitiously watching the door for Colin's arrival. Now as he entered, she felt his presence likc a physical forcc. Earlier she'd noticed that Mrs. Elberly had covered her crystals with a heavy velvet cloth. Good thing, she mused. Colin's presence would probably send them into a riot of disharmony. He certainly had that effect on her nerves.

Colin saw her standing in the corner talking to Mrs. Elberly. He hadn't wanted to come. Seeing Maggie disturbed him. Seeing her with Devin disturbed him even more. *Fool!* he chided himself.

Madaline had decided it would be best to keep her distance from Colin in public. Her reactions to him were too strong. But when she saw Devin approaching him, she excused herself from Mrs. Elberly and slowly made her way across the room toward the two men. *Don't get too close,* her inner voice warned as the mere memory of ministering to his hand caused a warming sensation in the pit of her stomach. Still, like a moth drawn to a flame, she continued toward him. She saw him nod as if agreeing with what Devin was telling him, then she saw him slip Devin the letter. Glancing around, she noticed that no one else in the room was paying any attention to the two men.

Suddenly Devin's voice grew louder. Not a great deal louder, but loud enough to carry to her, as well as to Helen and Ray, who were standing nearby. "My wife is too polite to say anything," Devin was saying, his voice taking on a reproving tone. "But she does not appreciate the attention you've been paying her. I'd like you to keep your association with her on a strictly professional basis."

Madaline froze. Devin was making it sound as if Colin had made an inappropriate pass as her.

Colin's face darkened in anger. What game was Mrs. Madaline MacGreggor-Smythe playing now? he wondered. He glanced toward her and saw the shock on her face. Clearly this had been Devin's idea. The man's trying to save his reputation, he thought. In a way he couldn't blame him, but he didn't like being made the patsy.

"Don't worry," he said, "You're welcome to your wife."

Madaline saw Helen and Joe glance her way. Colin had made it sound as if he considered her pure poison. She flushed with embarrassment. Tossing both of the men hostile glances, she stalked out of the room.

Devin caught up with her as she reached the car. "I'm sorry about what happened in there," he said. "I just couldn't help myself. I'm still not so sure Darnell isn't behind all of this.'

"I've never been so humiliated," she seethed. She'd also never felt so hurt, she thought, as she recalled the acid tone in Colin's voice. "I just want to go home," she finished curtly.

Devin apologized several times during the drive, but Madaline was still angry when they reached the house.

"I'm only trying to do what's best for you," Devin said as he parked the car.

"Maybe I'm tired of having you protecting me," she replied tersely.

Devin looked remorseful. "If you want, I'll go apologize to Colin."

Madaline recalled the ice in Colin's voice. "No, it wouldn't make any difference," she said tiredly. Then, excusing herself, she went up to her room.

Colin left the tea right after Devin and Maggie. No one had said anything about Devin's remark or Maggie's exit, but the stiltedness that had settled over the gathering grated on his nerves.

He drove back to Zebulon's place but he didn't go inside. Instead, he took the path up to the ridge. Standing there, looking out over the countryside, he told himself he should be relieved. Devin had informed him that he was going to hire a firm of detectives. "And that releases me from having to worry about Mrs. Madaline MacGreggor-Smythe any longer," he said aloud, as if saying it would make the statement true.

"You about ready to tell me what has you talking to yourself?" Zebulon asked from behind him.

Turning, Colin saw the old man entering the clearing.

"I've always made it a practice not to pry into other people's problems," Zebulon continued, seating himself on a boulder. "But you're like a son to me. It's been obvious since you came back to Smytheshire that there was something more than building a house on your mind. Been waiting for you to tell me. Now I'm asking, 'cause you look like a man who needs to talk to someone." His mouth formed a thoughtful pout. "'Course when I need to talk, I generally talk to old Buck here." He motioned with his cane toward his dog. "If you'd rather talk to him, I'll leave."

Colin shook his head. He wasn't about to tell Zebulon—or his dog—about Maggie. The subject was too personal, and he had too much pride. But ever since he'd learned about the hooded figure, he'd been thinking of doing a little investigating of his own.

"You ever hear of anyone in these parts playing around with old druid rituals?" he asked.

The old man studied him narrowly. "Now that is a right interesting question."

Colin had expected Zebulon to chuckle and ask where he'd gotten such a notion. But Zebulon wasn't laughing. "Then you *have* heard?" he said sharply.

"I ain't heard of anyone practicing any rituals," Zebulon replied, a grin spreading across his face. "But it sure would be something to think about if they was. Make old Angus Smythe roll over in his grave and shout, 'I told you so.'"

"You want to tell me what you're talking about?" Colin demanded, an uneasy feeling running along his spine at the mention of the Smythe name.

Zebulon was still shaking his head at the thought of how Angus Smythe would react. "Don't know if anyone else in this town knows the truth behind the founding of Smytheshire. If they do they aren't saying. 'Course I wouldn't know how they would have found out. Weren't never public knowledge. Fact is, only my family and the Smythes knew, and both families kept it pretty much a secret as far as I know. Truth is, I was beginning to think I was the only one who still remembered."

"What is this secret behind the founding of Smytheshire?" Colin prodded, his uneasiness growing.

Zebulon grinned mischievously. "Our druid heritage. At least seventy-five percent of the residents of our little community are descendants of families from whom the druid priesthood was chosen. You're one. I'm one. The Smythes are. Madaline MacGreggor is one, too."

"All of us?" Colin was having trouble believing this. He'd always thought of Zebulon as being a little eccentric, but he'd never thought the old man might be insane—not until this moment, anyway. "My parents never said anything to me about druid ancestry."

Zebulon frowned impatiently. "Like I told you, it's been kept a secret."

Colin continued to regard the old man dubiously. "According to all the histories I've ever read, the druids were killed off centuries ago. They didn't even leave any written records. The only reason we even know they existed is because they're mentioned in writings of other cultures and archaeologists have dug up a few remains."

"They never kept written records," Zebulon replied. "They stored all their knowledge in their heads in those days. And they weren't all killed. They simply went underground. At least those in Britain did and they're the ones we're all descended from. 'Course there weren't too many left and they were forced to disperse. It was too dangerous for them to stay together. They changed their names and spread out all over England and the continent. Secretly they kept in touch for the next few generations. But it was too dangerous to practice the old ways, and eventually most forgot about their druid ancestry and assimilated into whatever culture they'd fled to.

"But old Angus Smythe's ancestors kept track as good as they could of where the various families connected with the priesthood had gone. They also began to record the old rituals, stories, songs, whatever they could remember, before it was all forgotten. Sometime in the fifteen or sixteen hundreds, they decided to try to bring the descendants of those original families back together—somewhere near Manchester, England, I think. My memory isn't too good on this point. Anyway, some weren't interested in regathering. Religious beliefs were dangerous ground to tread on. Heretics were still being burned or hanged or worse. The Smythes had to move carefully, feel out the people before they could trust them. My family was one of the ones that felt the pull of the past and joined the regrouping. But the old mystical powers refused to be revived. Oh, there are stories of a few having some gifts of prophecy or a minor ability at healing, but nothing earth-shattering.

"Then whispers and rumors began to spread about the revival of the druid community. Again their lives were in danger. They fled to the New World sometime in the mid to late sixteen hundreds. But they were afraid of being persecuted even here, so they dispersed once again. And once again, most forgot their heritage and assimilated into the new culture. There were a few, including my family and the Smythes, who remained together for several generations in a small community up north of here. I'm not sure what happened, but sometime in the early eighteen hundreds, I think it was, they dispersed again. My grandfather, old Samuel Lansky, he was the one who told me what I know about our heritage, was a bit vague on dates. He wouldn't tell me what caused the breakup either. I got the impression our kin what were involved weren't too proud of having been a part of whatever it was and Granddad Samuel had decided it was time it were completely forgotten. Anyway, whatever happened it split the community apart. All the families went their separate ways. My people moved here and settled. The Smythes moved to Boston. Them and us were the only two families who stayed in contact.

"The Smythes had always been kinda wealthy. Through the next years, they increased their wealth until they no longer had to work for a living. And although the other families hadn't kept in touch with them, the Smythes continued to keep track of where the others had gone. Then one day Angus Smythe got it into his head to reassemble the druid community again. That was just before the turn of the century. He came to see my dad and my granddad.

Samuel didn't think it was a good idea. The old ways, he was sure, had died for good.

"But Angus was determined. Only this time, he got smart. He bought himself a big tract of land here and founded Smytheshire. That was in 1899, the same year I was born. That'd be ninety-three years ago come this June. Angus was a young man then, barely twenty-four. He found the descendants of the families that had come to America with his ancestors. He even managed to track down a few members of some of the families that had refused to join in the original regrouping and remained in Europe. He offered all of them jobs here in Smytheshire. Used a lot of different ploys to explain why he'd chosen them so's they wouldn't know he'd picked them special. If they wanted to own their own business, he offered loans to help them. And he was real careful not to come right out and mention their heritage.

"After he got them here, he sort of hinted around about druids and druid ways to see if he could spark any interest. But real quick it became clear that none of the people knew of their ancestry. Even more, they didn't want anything to do with what they viewed as sacrilegious cults. Still, Angus was sure that with so many gathered together in one spot, some spark would awaken the mystical forces within them, and their druid ancestry would again take over. But it never happened. At least not that I've heard." He studied Colin narrowly. "You know any differently?"

Colin shook his head. "I don't think there's any mystical powers involved, just someone playing a very distasteful game."

"Has something to do with that MacGreggor girl, don't it?" Zebulon asked. "I remember Grandpa Samuel got real excited when her grandparents moved to town. It was her grandmother that interested him, but he never told me why."

"It would seem that the women in Maggie's family have a way of unsettling men," Colin muttered.

It was early evening. Madaline paced the floor of her room. She couldn't relax. She was still furious with Devin for his behavior that afternoon. He'd embarrassed her and Colin.

"Colin will probably cross the street when he sees me coming from now on," she grumbled. But then he'd probably wanted to do that all along, she added regretfully.

A restlessness she couldn't control came over her. The thought that she might find some peace in the conservatory occurred to her. In rapid strides, she left the room. But when she reached the ground floor, she turned away from her sanctuary. Without even fully realizing where she was heading, she found herself outside the door of Devin's library. She frowned at herself as she knocked. She didn't really want to confront him just now. There was nothing she had to say to him. Even more, this room didn't just make her uneasy, she actually hated it. "My being here doesn't make any sense," she muttered under her breath. There was no answer to her knock. "What I need is a walk outside in the fresh air." But as if being forced forward by an inner instinct too strong to resist, she opened the door and entered.

The room seemed gloomier than usual. Quickly she flipped on the wall switch that lighted a large pewter chandelier suspended from the ceiling. Then she turned on every lamp. But even with the blaze of light, she had the sense of a shadow hanging over the room. Her gaze traveled to the books on the shelves. Many were first editions collected by Angus Smythe and his ancestors before him. He'd been a great lover of old books, and Devin had inherited that love. Devin's parents and his grandparents had not been so enthusiastic about these musty volumes, and when Devin had requested them, they'd gladly given them to him.

The subject matter varied, but horticulture seemed to have been a particular interest of the family for many generations. One entire wall was covered with volumes on the subject. Many of the books dealt with the medicinal qualities of plants, some highly scientific and some filled with nothing more than old wives' tales.

Like a magnet, her attention was drawn to some books on a high shelf. They were the ones Devin had been looking at the other day, she recalled. An uneasiness swept over her. A part of her wanted to run, but another part forced her legs to move toward that side of the library. Positioning the ladder, she climbed up for a closer look. Her foreboding grew with each step.

As she reached the level of the shelf, her gaze focused on one particular volume. Like the others surrounding it, it was old, very old. The leather binding showed signs of age and heavy usage. A chill ran along her spine. Even before she pulled it out, she knew what it was. Her hand shook as she touched it.

It was the handwritten book she had seen on the seat of Colin's truck.

"I'm surprised to find you in here."

She jerked around, nearly losing her balance. Devin was standing near the center of the room watching her. He'd closed the door and she felt as if she were suddenly being smothered.

"You staged the scene on the ridge," she said accusingly, knowing with every fiber of her being that this was so.

"True," he confessed with no sign of remorse or apology.

"Why?" she demanded, anger overcoming her fear.

"Because you have a destiny to fulfill," he replied. "Old Angus Smythe died when I was barely nine, but among his books, he left me this diary."

He had moved toward his desk. He tapped a small old very worn leather volume lying there and said, "He and I had talked a great deal about our druid heritage. He was a patient man, willing to sit by and wait and hope for a rebirth of the powers our people once possessed. My father and grandfather feel the same." He frowned. "Actually I'm not sure they really believe there is any power left. But they're wrong. The power is still within us. And, my great-grandfather was wrong, too. Patience is not the answer. I've always known I was special, that I had been born to perform some great act. This diary showed me the path to take. Your ancestor's betrayal of all we were is chronicled in here. She was the chosen one, yet she ran away rather than accept the highest of all honors that had been placed upon her. Your ancestor was to have died, her life offered to the elements of nature, and by her death, given us a rebirth. When you were born my great-grandfather was certain our powers would be rekindled and you would be the key."

This was a Devin Madaline had never seen before. His jaw was set with purpose and there was an insane gleam in his eyes. She looked toward the door, calculating her chances of reaching it. She could probably make it. But if he'd locked it...

Screaming for help would be smart, she decided. "Mrs. Grayson," she yelled at the top of her lungs. Remembering the day staff, she added, "Paula! Lynn!"

"This room is soundproof," Devin said softly. "Besides, Mrs. Grayson and Claire have gone into town on an errand for me. And I sent the rest of the staff home a little early. I could see how upset you were, and it occurred to me that I might need to keep you here by force. I had hoped to allow you your freedom for a day longer, but Colin seems to have a most disturbing effect on you. I can't trust you to stay away from him, and your virginity is of grave importance."

Madaline's stomach knotted. "My virginity?"

"The sacrifice must be pure," he replied. "And believe me, assuring that hasn't been easy. Luckily for me, no other man but Colin has ever really interested you. But I was always worried. Then your mother became ill. I knew you were desperate for her to receive the very best care. That opened up a new possibility. I invented the story about my grandfather insisting that I marry. All I had to do was keep you pure until the May of your twenty-fifth year. That was the age of your ancestor when she betrayed us. I was sure my ultimate goal would allow me to play my role with ease. But you're a very appealing woman. Living here under the same roof with you and pretending to be impotent has been a strain."

She stared at him in disbelief. "You're *not* impotent?" she said, trying to assimilate everything he was saying.

"No." He smiled as if pleased with himself. "But the subterfuge was necessary and it worked beautifully. It gave me a reason to marry you and still maintain your virginity. And you felt a sympathy toward me that bonded us closer."

Madaline couldn't believe what a fool she had been. Then a spark of hope ignited. "Whoever wrote those notes must know about this game you've been playing."

Devin grinned. "I wrote those notes. I needed a little something to make you act on edge, to give Mrs. Grayson the notion that you were frightened of something or someone. I used the virginity angle because I knew you wouldn't want to betray my trust and your concern for my feelings would cause you to want to keep the reason for your uneasiness a secret." He breathed a wistful sigh.

"You have such a strong sense of loyalty. I'm going to miss that."

"But why send Colin a note and bring him into this?" Madaline asked, still confused. *You're dealing with a madman,* she reminded herself.

"Colin must pay for an injustice done to me. He once rescued a small dog that had bitten me. The dog deserved to die. Now I intend to see that Colin suffers in its place." His manner was coolly calculating. "Besides, I needed someone to frame for your murder and he's the perfect scapegoat. He'd never married. I couldn't be certain if his experience with you had caused him to distrust women or if he still harbored some feelings for you. Either way, I was confident that if I could get him here, I could make it look as if he was pursuing you against your will. If the note hadn't worked, I would have come up with another ploy." He smiled with self-approval. "Besides, I couldn't waste all the preparation I'd done on Mrs. Grayson. Four years ago, when you and Colin first discovered the strength of your attraction for each other, I began to plant the seed of dislike for him in her mind."

Madaline recalled how Mrs. Grayson had shown disapproval of Colin even then. "But Colin hasn't pursued me since his arrival back in town. In fact, it's been just the opposite."

"Not in Mrs. Grayson's eyes," Devin pointed out.

Madaline's mind flashed back through the encounters with Colin in this house, beginning with the night he'd been outside the conservatory. Her stomach tightened with fear for him.

"Mrs. Grayson will swear the man has been harassing you," Devin finished with confidence. "And my performance at the tea this afternoon should have already set a few tongues wagging."

Madaline knew he was right. She glanced toward the door again. She would have to make a run for it. Her hand closed around one of the heavier volumes. "Devin, you can't really want to harm me. You've always promised to protect me," she said, attempting to reason with him one last time.

"And I have," he replied. "You should not be afraid. Your death will be a new beginning, not an end."

Not the kind of new beginning she wanted, she retorted mentally. Pulling the book out, Madaline hurled it at him. Then she jumped down from the ladder and dashed for the door. But as she reached for the knob, a hand closed around her arm and she felt something prick her flesh. Suddenly the world was spinning, then a blackness enveloped her.

She awoke groggily. Her arms and legs ached, but when she tried to stretch, she was inhibited. As she came to her senses, she realized that she was bound at the wrists and ankles with a single length of rope, a style used to bind calves at rodeos. Making her position more painful, her legs and arms were behind her with her hands and feet barely more than a foot apart.

"I apologize for the discomfort," Devin said. "But you will not have to endure it for long. Tomorrow is May first, the day you rectify the traitorous act of your ancestor and give birth once again to the powers lying dormant within our people."

Her gaze following the sound of his voice, she saw him standing a few feet away. He towered above her, and she realized she was lying on the floor. A light fixture on the ceiling gave illumination to the room. Actually it wasn't large enough to call a room, she decided. It was more the size of a walk-in closet. Her gaze traveled around the small enclosure. There were no furnishings. But on the wall was a row of wooden pegs. Hanging from one of them was the hooded cape she had seen the figure on the ridge wearing. On another peg hung a leather sheath housing the knife that looked so much like Colin's. And there were bunches of mistletoe hanging from the ceiling in every corner of the room.

"Mistletoe is a very honored plant," Devin said, noticing the direction of her gaze. "Ralph Snider almost killed my most precious species, but I managed to salvage it." Promise glistened in his eyes. "One day I'll see that he pays dearly for the harm he attempted to do."

Mentally Madaline kicked herself for not doing some research on druids and druid customs. But she had wanted to forget everything about the hooded figure on the ridge. Her attention returned to Devin. *He's totally slipped over the edge,* she thought frantically. "Where am I?" she asked. She knew the answer would do her no good, but she at least wanted to know where she was going to die.

"You're in my private sanctuary," he replied. "It's a secret room behind one of the walls of books in the library. The builder my father hired to construct this house was a man who liked money and understood a man's need for privacy. He was extremely agreeable to secretly adding this little addition for me. In the floor plans it appears as an alcove meant to house my herbarium. I convinced Mr. Colburn to come in by himself after all the initial work was done and create this room for me." Devin breathed a mock sigh of regret. "He carried the secret to his grave."

Madaline knew without a doubt that he'd aided in the man's demise. She recalled that Avery Colburn had been killed in a car crash. Devin had been merely eighteen at the time. Fear knotted her stomach tighter.

Devin smiled. "Of course everyone thinks you're on your way to our cabin in Maine. I've told Mrs. Grayson that Colin called while she and Claire were out and that the call upset you so much you felt you needed to get away from him. Tomorrow night after the ceremony, I'll take your body up to the ridge. The next morning I'll raise the alarm. I'll be concerned because I will have discovered you never reached your destination. Chief Brant will find your car hidden in a grove of trees outside of town. He'll also find a blanket with your blood on it in the back of Colin's car."

He frowned thoughtfully. "I was worried for a moment when Colin hurt his hand. I couldn't afford to have him injured too badly. That might lead to some question of him being able to do the foul deed." His smile returned. "However, he's fit enough."

Devin moved toward her. "As I've done on many occasions, I slipped a bit of sedative into Mrs. Grayson's and Claire's evening tea to ensure they sleep soundly. Now just to make certain you get a good night's rest and I don't have to worry about you..."

She saw the syringe in his hand and tried to pull away. "Who was the hooded figure I saw kill the rabbit?" she asked, trying to find something to talk about that would delay the injection.

He paused. "It was Harvey Clark. He was furious with Colin and eager to help me. Afterward, I couldn't trust him to keep quiet, so I had to arrange that little accident for him."

Madaline recalled that, like Avery Colburn, Harvey Clark had died in a car crash. It had happened just a week or so after she'd gone back to school following that fateful summer.

"I can't believe how completely you've had me and everyone else in this town fooled," she said, amazed that the Devin she thought she'd known could have cloaked such an insane mind. Her brow wrinkled in puzzled consternation. "And I can't believe I didn't realize that hooded figure wasn't Colin,'' she added, furious with herself for not noticing something that would have made her question the figure's identity. Her frown deepened. This oversight didn't make sense. She had been so acutely aware of Colin she didn't even usually have to turn around when he entered a room to know he was there.

Devin grinned rakishly. "I confess, I drugged you. I'm rather proud of the concoction. It's something I created myself from my plants—a sort of hallucinogen. It put you into a mild hypnotic state, which allowed me to tell you what you were seeing and, with just a few props, convince you that you were seeing Colin performing a druid ritual. It also allowed me to build a fear in you that caused you to stay away from Colin. I couldn't take the chance he might make you doubt it was him on the ridge.'' He shook his head. "But your mind has grown stronger these past years. I tried it again the last couple of nights in the hot chocolate, but you refused to doubt Colin this time.'' He smiled. "You will make an excellent sacrifice.'' Again he moved toward her. "And now it's late and I must get a few hours' sleep.''

As she felt the needle prick her arm, Madaline's mind screamed out to Colin. I'm the last person he'd come dashing to rescue, she chided herself as the shot took effect and the blackness overtook her.

Chapter Twelve

Colin sat bolt upright in bed. A cold sweat broke out on his forehead and the palms of his hands as he stared into the darkness. He could have sworn he'd heard Maggie call out to him, but there was no one there. Fear for her pervaded him. It was just a dream, he told himself. But he'd never had a dream that seemed so real.

He had an overwhelming urge to phone her and assure himself that she was all right. But then he remembered that not only was it the middle of the night, she was Devin's wife. Suddenly the image of Maggie tending his injured hand filled his mind and he recalled the vulnerable expression on her face. "Well, she can't expect to have her cake and eat it, too," he growled. He drew a frustrated breath and ordered himself back to sleep. But sleep didn't come easily and, when it did, it was a restless slumber filled with foreboding images of Maggie imprisoned in a dark room.

"You look like hell," Zebulon remarked as he and Colin sat eating breakfast the next morning.

"I feel like it," Colin confessed. "Had a whole slew of nightmares about Maggie. But the woman doesn't need my help. She has a husband who can provide her with the best protection money can buy. No reason for me to concern myself with her any longer."

Zebulon was studying him thoughtfully. "Could be you don't have a choice."

Colin had to admit that was how he felt. As hard as he tried to put her out of his mind, fear for her lingered. Irritated with his weakness, he frowned at Zebulon. "Of course I have a choice. And she had a choice, and she chose Devin." He clamped his mouth shut. That was the closest he had ever come to letting his jealousy show in front of Zebulon. He scowled at the thought of the sympathy he expected to see on the old man's face. But there was no sign of it.

Instead, Zebulon continued to study Colin speculatively, and then said, "My grandfather once told me that there were legends about some of our ancestors being 'connected.' Sort of like ESP. They could transmit thoughts—send out warnings to one another or cries for help. Could be that you and the MacGreggor girl have that. Maybe it just took a few years to mature or maybe she *is* in danger and that's the spark necessary to set it off."

"That's a bunch of nonsense," Colin growled. Just the thought of being "connected" to Maggie shook him. He had come here to get her out of his system not to discover that there was a possibility she might haunt him forever. Abruptly he recalled the time when she was around twelve and had gotten herself stuck on the roof of her parents' house. He'd known she was in trouble. He'd known it! *What I knew was that I'd left a ladder where a child could use it to get hurt,* he told himself curtly. But as he pushed that memory to the back of his mind, the incident with Harvey Clark came forward. When Harvey had grabbed Maggie, Colin had felt her fear like a sharp jolt. *I merely made a reasonable assumption that he had frightened her,* he corrected.

"There seems to be something between you and Madaline MacGreggor," Zebulon persisted.

"There *was* some unfinished business," Colin replied. "But it's finished now." He rose from the table to signal that he considered this subject closed. But as he carried his dishes to the sink, his apprehension refused to go away.

Deciding that hard labor would help to get Maggie out of his mind, he went up to the ridge and began working on repairing the foundation. But by nine, he had to admit defeat.

"You're a danger to yourself today," Ray Kolby remarked.

Colin cursed the pain he'd just suffered by hitting his thumb with a hammer. He couldn't deny Ray's comment. Earlier he'd scratched his arm deep enough to cause it to bleed. And it was all Maggie's fault. Her image was constantly interrupting his concentration. "I have a phone call I have to make," he said, and strode off toward Zebulon's house.

There he dialed Maggie's office number. Samantha answered and informed him that Mrs. Smythe had gone on a short vacation.

"It was just a nightmare," he muttered to himself as he hung up. "Nothing more than an overactive imagination." But as he headed back toward the ridge, a part of him insisted that Maggie was still in Smytheshire.

A little while later, when the chain saw he was using to cut up the trunk of a fallen tree slipped and nearly cut him, he could no longer deny his continuing apprehension.

"I've got some business to take care of in town," he informed the Kolbys. He noticed with dry amusement that they both seemed relieved to see him leaving.

"No reason to hurry back," John called after him, confirming his suspicion.

"That woman is going to be the death of me," Colin muttered. This thought was supposed to cause anger and exasperation. Instead, a cold chill ran along his spine as if those words were closer to the truth than he thought. "This druid mumbo-jumbo has my nerves on edges," he grumbled as he drove toward town.

Passing through Smytheshire, he continued on to Devin's home. He felt like an idiot as he knocked on the front door.

"Mrs. Smythe is away," Mrs. Grayson informed him coolly when he asked to see Maggie.

He didn't doubt that the woman believed what she was saying. But he could swear he felt Maggie's presence nearby.

"Is something wrong?" Devin asked, coming up behind the housekeeper.

Mrs. Grayson had not allowed Colin into the house. "He's looking for Mrs. Smythe," she said, stepping aside so that Devin could take her place in the doorway. "I've told him she's not here."

Devin frowned impatiently at Colin. "I thought I made it plain that my wife does not want you bothering her."

Colin noticed Mrs. Grayson's look of approval. That, plus the insinuation in Devin's voice that his presence was a nuisance to Maggie, caused a sharp jab of irritation. It was her presence in his mind that was the nuisance! And right now that presence was stronger than ever.

"I need to see your wife on business," Colin said tersely. "After all, she did sign a contract to be the architect on my home." His jaw tensed. "I know she's here."

"You're wrong. She is not here. But when she calls, I'll tell her you came by," Devin replied with dismissal. Then he stepped back inside and closed the door.

Colin scowled at the barrier. He could have sworn he saw a moment of panic in Devin's eyes. The urge to break down the door and search the house was close to overwhelming. "And I'd probably be making a complete fool of myself," he growled under his breath. Of course Devin looked panicked. He didn't want to lose his inheritance. And if everyone was lying about Maggie being out of town, it was most likely on her orders. It took an effort, but he forced himself to walk back to his car.

From inside the house, Devin watched Colin. It was as if Colin actually knew Madaline was still there, he thought. It had never occurred to him that the two of them could be connected. He frowned at himself. This was a complication he hadn't expected. But if she was dead, Colin wouldn't be able to sense her presence any longer. The ceremony would have to be performed quickly.

He turned to Mrs. Grayson with a beseeching smile. "I was wondering if you and Claire would mind doing the grocery shopping before lunch," he said. "I've gotten a sudden craving for some fried oysters."

Mrs. Grayson looked mildly surprised, but she smiled kindly. "Of course," she said. "I guess being driven to eat by that man is better than being driven to drink."

Devin smiled back. The two women were the only people here at the estate. He had wanted as few people around today as possible in order to prepare himself properly for the ceremony. To accomplish this, he'd sent his head gardener, Charles Henley, and Charles's assistant to Mrs. Elberly's house to tidy up her yard and put some fresh plantings in to cheer up the woman. And he'd sent the two day maids to her home with instructions to give it a thorough cleaning. He'd told them that when they were done, they could take the rest of the day off. His smile deepened when he recalled how everyone had commented on how thoughtful he was. Yes, he admitted. He was very thoughtful. And when the power that lay dormant within them began to come to life, they would think even more highly of him.

After seeing Claire and Mrs. Grayson off, he went into the kitchen and took one of the seedcakes Claire had baked the day before. His self-satisfied smile broadened.

Madaline was awake when Devin returned. She'd been struggling against her bonds but to no avail.

After entering the room, he took down the belt holding the sheathed knife and fastened it around his waist. Then he took the hooded cloak from its peg and put it on. As he approached her he said, "I've brought you a bit of a treat." He eased her up into a kneeling position, and removed her gag.

She immediately began to scream.

"Even if this room wasn't soundproof, there is no one nearby to hear you," he assured her. "You are, however, giving me a headache. So either be quiet or I'll put the gag back in."

The thought of having the filthy rag stuffed back into her mouth made Madaline shut up.

"I know you've never liked these little seedcakes. But I'm quite proud of them. They're my own recipe."

Madaline had known this. Claire called them Devin's health cakes. They were made with coarse flours from grains he grew here on the estate and ground himself.

"In the past I've never forced one on you, but today I must insist you eat a portion of one." He broke a piece off the one he was holding. "This piece," he said.

Madaline noticed a curious marking burned into the bite he thrust toward her.

"It's the sign of the chosen one," he said, noticing the line of her vision.

Madaline clamped her mouth shut.

"It's not going to harm you to eat it," Devin coaxed. As if to prove to her that the cake was safe, he took a bite from the portion that had no burned markings.

Madaline kept her mouth clamped shut. If she was going to die, at least she would die without that bland-tasting bread in her mouth and a heathen sign digesting in her stomach.

Devin's smile vanished. "You're trying my patience," he warned. "I would hate to have to force this into you, but I will."

Playing for time, Madaline took a small bite. She chewed it grudgingly and very, very slowly.

"Swallow," he ordered.

The urge to spit it at him was strong, but prudence suggested that, rather than infuriate him more, it might be best to humor him for a while. He might relax his guard and provide her with an opportunity to escape. Still her throat contracted, rebelling against actually swallowing the coarse cake. "My throat's too dry to swallow," she protested.

Furious, he stalked out of the room. Again she struggled against her bonds. But when he returned a few moments later she was still securely bound.

He held a glass of water to her mouth.

She took a drink and swallowed.

"Another bite," he ordered, holding the charred piece of seedcake toward her once again.

Madaline obeyed. As she chewed, she felt more and more doomed with each passing second. Colin's image filled her mind. She could not allow his life to be destroyed because of her. She must find some way of providing a clue to the police that Devin was her true murderer.

"Swallow," he ordered.

When she did, he laid the remainder of the bread aside. "And now it is time for you to fulfill your destiny."

Madaline's mind was beginning to feel hazy. He'd tricked her again. He'd drugged her piece of the cake. Idiot! she screamed at herself. She tried to scream aloud, but her facial muscles and vocal cords refused to work properly. Only the barest strangled cry came out.

"You will feel only a modicum of pain and then it will be over," he promised as he untied her.

She tried to fight him, but the drug had sapped her of most of her strength and robbed her of the ability to command the muscles of her legs and arms. She concentrated on Colin's image. As Devin lifted her to her feet, her hand closed around a button on the shirt he was wearing under the cloak. Focusing all the strength she could muster into her fingers, she ripped the button off as he tossed her over his shoulder. *Don't open your fist,* she ordered herself as he carried her out of the house.

An image of Maggie at the mercy of the hooded figure flashed through Colin's mind. "I'm letting my imagination get the better of me," he thought as he left Smytheshire behind, heading back to Zebulon's place. Hadn't Devin always protected her? And he was sure Mrs. Grayson wouldn't do her any harm.

But even as his rational mind told him he was being a fool, his foot hit the brake. In the next minute, he'd turned his car around and was driving back toward Devin's. On Birch Street he passed Claire and Mrs. Grayson going in the opposite direction. Again the hooded figure flashed into his mind. A sudden panic filled him and he floored the accelerator.

Reaching Devin's house, he slammed on his brakes, jumped out of the car and raced for the front door. Grabbing the large iron knocker, he banged it forcefully. He didn't care if he was making a fool of himself. He was going to search every inch of this place.

There was no answer. He tried the door. It was locked. The thought that he could easily break in through the conservatory entered his mind. *You're behaving like a lunatic,* he told himself as he raced around the house.

Devin carried Madaline to the center of the herb garden set in the midst of the oak grove. As he placed her in a kneeling position beside the birdbath that formed the focal point, the arrangement of this garden struck her fully. The birdbath was not a typical birdbath. It had been created from a large boulder. The sides of the boulder had been chipped away until the rock was shaped into the form of a crude vase. The top had been hollowed out enough to hold a small pool of water. At the moment, however, the water had been poured out of the basin and wood and leaves had been placed within the cavity. Her stomach knotted as she realized that the stone benches, spaced at intervals within the arrangement of trees and plants, created a circle of stones around this central altar.

She shoved the fist holding the button into her pocket, using the fabric pouch to force her hand to remain closed around the one bit of evidence she hoped would save Colin. Then her mind focused on her and her fate. She refused to die without one final attempt to save herself. Running or fighting was out of the question. Her legs and arms felt like putty. One last good scream, she decided, filling her lungs with air...

Colin had reached the back lawn when he heard it. It was faint, almost beyond perception, but he was certain he'd heard a strangled cry. His attention shifted to the gardens beyond the back lawn. Frantic, he raced in the direction from which the cry had come.

Devin clamped his hand over Madaline's mouth. "I told you there was no one around to save you," he said impatiently. "You should be honored. This is a new beginning, the rebirth of an ancient culture."

Silently Madaline told him what she thought of this honor. It involved words she would never use aloud. Then her teeth closed around the fleshy part of his hand and she bit down hard.

"Ouch!" he yelped, releasing her.

She was fighting the drug and winning, she realized with a flush of triumph. Again she screamed. It wasn't loud, more like a weak cry, but it was something.

He struck her, knocking her over. "You're only making this more difficult for yourself."

I'm trying to make it more difficult for you, her mind responded, but the blow had left her too stunned to form this sentence aloud.

Colin reached the perimeter of the herb garden just as the hooded figure struck Maggie. Every fiber of his being wanted to grab whoever was wearing that brown robe and kill him with his bare hands.

He rushed forward. "What's going on here?" he demanded, purposely diverting the hooded person's attention away from Maggie.

Madaline's heart gave a lurch at the sound of Colin's voice. He had come to her rescue once again!

Devin spun around. "What are you doing here!" he screamed. "Get off my property!"

Colin blinked in surprise at the realization of who the hooded figure was. Then he read the insanity in Devin's eyes. "I'll be happy to leave, but I'm taking Maggie with me." He still wanted to punch Devin, but getting Maggie out of there was his first priority.

"You're not taking her anywhere," Devin snarled. His hand went to the sheath beneath the cloak.

Terror for Colin filled Madaline. "Watch out! Dangerous...knife!" she managed to choke out, as Colin neared her and reached down toward her.

Colin spun around just as Devin's hand emerged holding the knife with Colin's initials carved in the handle.

"Mr. Devin!"

It was Mrs. Grayson's voice. Madaline looked past the two men to see the housekeeper and the cook come to an abrupt halt at the edge of the clearing.

"I saw Mr. Darnell driving back in this direction and insisted that Claire turn the car around and follow him," Mrs. Grayson was saying, clearly having trouble comprehending the scene before her. "We thought he might have come to harm you." Her voice had faded into a disbelieving whisper as her gaze traveled from the knife to Madaline, who was lying limply on the ground.

"I'm doing this for you, for all of you!" Devin shouted. "It's your heritage. It was Madaline's ancestor who robbed us of our power by running away, instead of offering herself unselfishly for sacrifice. Now I am undoing that wrong."

Colin stared at him grimly. "You're insane."

Madaline attempted to rise, but her actions were slow and painful.

Devin glanced down at her. "You'll not escape this time," he swore, ignoring Colin and lunging at her with the knife.

Colin caught Devin's arm, and in the next instant both men were on the ground struggling with one another.

"Help Colin," Madaline called out weakly to the two women standing on the edge of the garden. But still clearly shocked and confused by what was happening, neither moved. Sheer willpower helped Madaline move out of the men's way. Her gaze never leaving them, she tried to position herself so that she could aid Colin if the opportunity arose.

Devin fought like the madman he was. He slashed at Colin, cutting Colin's arm. For a moment, Colin loosened his hold.

Devin was instantly on his feet. "Once Madaline is dead I shall have the power to defeat all my enemies!" he bellowed, again lunging toward her. But his foot caught in the root of the oldest oak of the grove. Losing his balance, he fell forward.

He issued a yell of surprise, followed by a gasp. Then he lay silent.

For a long moment, no one moved. Then Mrs. Grayson slowly entered the clearing, followed by Claire. As Madaline sat poised to defend herself should Devin suddenly rise, and Colin watched, holding his bleeding arm, Mrs. Grayson touched Devin's cheek.

"Mr. Devin," she said cautiously. Then her complexion paled and she stepped back.

It was Claire who turned Devin over. The knife had gone through his heart.

Colin drew a breath of relief. Walking over to Madaline, he knelt beside her. "I'll get you a doctor," he said.

"I'm...just drugged," she managed. He was safe. That was what mattered most to her. Unable to stop herself, she reached out and gently stroked his jaw. "You're...the one who needs... a doctor."

Her touch left a trail of fire. Colin wanted to take her in his arms, then he reminded himself of why she was there in the first place. "Looks like you weren't as smart as you thought you were in your choice of men," he said gruffly.

His contempt hurt. She wanted to defend herself, but the drug made talking difficult. Besides, he probably wouldn't believe her, anyway.

"Mrs. Grayson, Mrs. Smythe will be needing you," Colin said with command. His attention shifted to Claire. "Would you call a doctor and the police?" he requested in a manner that was more an order than a suggestion. Then, with his good arm, he hoisted Madaline over his shoulder and carried her toward the house.

The feel of her ignited a warmth in him. The urge to continue with her to his car and take her back to Zebulon's place was strong. *She's nothing but trouble,* he reminded himself curtly. *The smart thing to do would be to get rid of her as quickly as possible.*

Madaline felt the tenseness in his muscles. Glancing sideways, she saw the grim line of his jaw and knew he didn't like being this close to her. She couldn't blame him. When he'd saved her from Harvey Clark's unwelcome advances, he'd ended up with a broken nose and two black eyes. This time he'd nearly been killed. He'd probably be happy if he never saw her again, she thought. She was given further proof of this as he carried her into her room, placed her on her bed and then walked out without a backward glance.

Madaline awoke the next morning in the bedroom that had been hers since childhood. After she'd given Chief Brant her statement about what had happened and answered all his questions, she'd refused to remain in Devin's house a moment longer. Satisfied she would be all right on her own, Dr. James had driven her home. Before leaving the estate, she'd given her wedding and engagement rings to Mrs. Grayson to give to Devin's parents. Then she'd asked the housekeeper to pack her things and send them to her. She never wanted to cross that threshold again.

Glancing toward the window, she saw the sun just breaking over the horizon. Her gaze shifted to the table beside her bed. On it lay the only thing she had taken from Devin's house that was not hers. It was the diary containing the history of her ancestor. She wasn't certain what she was going to do with it, but she did know she was going to be very careful about whom she allowed to see it.

Rising, she dressed in a pair of old jeans and a sweatshirt. Colin Darnell filled her mind as she went downstairs to the kitchen to make herself some coffee. She wanted to see him so badly it hurt. Passing by the hall mirror, she paused and glanced at herself. She looked as if she'd been in a brawl. Her wrists and ankles were bandaged and she had bruises and scrapes on her face. "He wouldn't want to see me," she muttered with a grimace. Breathing a tired sigh, she added, "He wouldn't even want to see me if I looked my best."

But as she continued on to the kitchen, she stopped abruptly. The biggest mistake of her life had been not facing Colin four years ago. "Am I willing to let him go without a fight?" she asked herself. Her jaw firmed. *No!* came the answer.

Colin awoke before dawn. He'd slept restlessly. After Maggie had told her story to the police, Chief Brant had taken Colin's statement. Colin and Thatcher Brant were old friends, and Thatcher had been willing to share the details of Maggie's story with him. Now all the loose ends were tied up.

"It's over," he told himself as he rose and dressed. He could go back to Boston as soon as he'd talked to the Kolby brothers and let them know he was leaving the rest of the work on the house in their and Maggie's care.

Not "Maggie," he reminded himself grimly as he climbed to the ridge. Dawn had just broken, but he'd been too tense to sit around Zebulon's house and wait until it was time for the men to begin arriving for work. She was and always had been Madaline MacGreggor-Smythe. Still, he found himself wishing that even just a small part of his Maggie existed.

Madaline found him sitting on a boulder just as he had been the first time she'd come up to the ridge. Only that time, he was the one who looked as if he'd been in a brawl. Self-consciously, her hand went up to her face. But the icy expression in his eyes as he looked up at her approach caused her to drop her hand back to her side. Her appearance would make no difference to him. Clearly he'd be happy if he never saw her again. The urge to turn and run was strong, but she forced herself to continue into the clearing.

"Zebulon said he thought I could find you here," she said, breaking the silence between them. "I wanted to thank you for saving my life."

Dressed in those jeans and that sweatshirt, she looked like his Maggie, Colin thought. *But she's not,* he reminded himself. "You're welcome." *Tell her you're leaving her and the Kolby brothers in charge of building the house,* he ordered himself. She could pass the message on and he'd be free to leave immediately. Instead, he heard himself saying, "Guess you had quite a scare. But inheriting Devin's money should ease your pain."

"I won't be inheriting any of Devin's estate," she said levelly. "I married him for his money, but it wasn't for me. It was for my mother. I wanted her to have the very best of medical care." She flushed under the sudden intense scrutiny of his gaze. "Guess that sounds kind of hokey, but it's the truth."

He wanted to believe her so much it hurt. "Why didn't you tell me that in the first place?" he demanded.

"Pride," she replied tightly. Her jaw tensed. Pride was telling her to leave now before she made a complete fool of herself. Instead, her shoulders squared. He was worth fighting for. "I insisted Devin had a prenuptial agreement drawn up that said I would leave the marriage with only what was mine."

Colin studied her. That sounded like his Maggie. But there was still the matter of trust. Until this moment he had refused to admit, even to himself, how deeply her rejection had hurt him. When she'd suddenly, without any explanation, refused even to speak to him, it was as if she had reached inside him and ripped out a part of him. He wouldn't set himself up for that kind of pain again.

"None of this would have happened if you'd come to me four years ago and allowed me to defend myself," he said rawly.

The depth of accusation in his voice shook her. This isn't working, she told herself. Still she could not give up. She had come this far. She would see it to the end.

"That wasn't entirely my fault. Devin had drugged me. I saw what he wanted me to see, and the drug also helped him create a fear in me that caused me to be terrified of you." She was watching Colin, looking for any sign that what she was telling him was making any difference. But his gaze remained shuttered. "If it's any consolation, the drug didn't work when he tried it this time," she finished.

The plea in her eyes tore at Colin. He was finding it difficult to think clearly. But he didn't want her to play him for the fool again. The intensity of his feelings for her still scared him.

Hot tears burned behind her eyes as his silence continued. Defeat washed over her. He either didn't believe her or he didn't care. Her back stiffened. She still had some pride left. She would not beg him to give her another chance. Turning away, she started down the hill.

Even as he told himself it might be wisest to let her go, he couldn't bear to see her walking away. He was on his feet in an instant. He wanted to believe her. He *needed* to believe her. He *did* believe her.

His hand closed around her arm, stopping her retreat. "Maggie," he said harshly.

Her jaw trembled as she turned to look at him. What if he offered her sympathy but said he could never care for her like he once had? She steeled herself for the worst.

"It occurs to me that you need a husband, one who will make certain that virginity is no longer hazardous to your health," he continued gruffly.

"That seems reasonable," she replied. Her stomach knotted with fear that she might be misinterpreting his meaning as she forced herself to ask, "Do you have anyone in mind?"

The anxiety he saw in her eyes stunned him. There was pain there, too, a pain that mirrored his own. He knew then that their separation had been as hurtful to her as it had been to him.

"I know I can be difficult," he said. "But I was wondering if you might consider me?"

Joy filled her and her hands went up to cup his face gently. "I've never honestly considered anyone else," she admitted.

"I love you, Maggie. I always have," he confessed, drawing her into his embrace and holding her tightly. For the first time in four years, he felt whole.

"And I love you, Colin Darnell," she replied, the heat of his body pervading hers until she felt as if she was wrapped in a blanket of warmth.

* * *

A week later, Madaline awoke in Colin's apartment in Boston. She was in Colin's arms. She smiled contentedly as she lifted her left hand and gazed at the simple gold band on her third finger.

Colin had been lying quietly, holding her and watching her. Now he grinned with satisfaction at the look of pleasure he saw on her face. "At the wedding, Zebulon told me that he's not a great believer in marriage, but in our case figured it was inevitable."

Madaline glanced at her new husband dubiously. "Inevitable?"

"He refuses to believe that I guessed you were in danger because subconsciously my mind was putting together all the pieces of the puzzle. He's sure we're 'connected.'"

"Well, I definitely feel 'connected' to you," she replied, smiling once again at her wedding ring. Then as ugly memories assailed her, she frowned. "However, I really don't want to discuss our druid heritage." She ran her hand over his hair-roughened chest as the fires of desire ignited within her. "At least not right now."

"I can find much better ways to spend our time, too," he said huskily, drawing her close. But as he lifted his head to kiss her, he caught a glimpse of the small leather-bound volume on the bedside table. Pausing, he looked down at her. "There is just one thing I'd like to know."

"And what's that?" she asked, playfully running her hands along his back.

"Are we going to continue to carry that diary with us everywhere we go?"

Madaline flushed. "No. I'd like to burn it, but Chief Brant suggested I hold on to it for a while. I thought you could put it away in your safe-deposit box."

"Done!" he agreed.

A thoughtful expression came over Madaline's face. "I realize that everyone who knows the whole story about Devin's death has agreed that the less said about this matter the better, but I think I'll write my cousin. She's had some unusual experiences in her life, and knowing about her heritage might help her understand them better."

"I certainly hope you don't plan to write that letter right now," Colin said, dipping his head and kissing her neck.

"Definitely not right now," she assured him.

* * * * *

Watch for HAUNTED HUSBAND,
Elizabeth August's next installment in the
Smytheshire, Massachusetts series.
Coming in February from Silhouette Romance.